Anonymous

Uncle John's third Book

Anonymous

Uncle John's third Book

ISBN/EAN: 9783337398903

Printed in Europe, USA, Canada, Australia, Japan

Cover: Foto ©Andreas Hilbeck / pixelio.de

More available books at **www.hansebooks.com**

UNCLE JOHN'S

THIRD BOOK.

Illustrated with numerous Engravings.

NEW YORK:

D. APPLETON & CO., 443 & 445 BROADWAY.

1865.

PREFACE TO UNCLE JOHN'S THIRD BOOK.

DEAR LITTLE CHILDREN:

HAVE you read Uncle John's First and Second Books? Have you looked at all the pretty pictures, and learned all the stories about them? Has your dear mother, sister, or aunt taken you upon her knee, and read to you all the little tales which are in the books, or are you such good studious children, that you can take a book yourself and read, when there are no long words to twist up your dear little tongues, and puzzle your dear little brains? Perhaps you have read the two volumes through many times, till you

can tell the story to every picture to your
baby brothers and sisters. If so, I am sure
you are ready for some new tales and pictures,
tales full of sweet thoughts, and words to
make you love gentleness and truth, pictures
that will teach you something new worth
learning. And so, knowing that to a good
child there is no present so valuable as a
new book, Uncle John offers you his Third
Book, full of fresh stories and pictures. As
he hopes you have studied hard, and learned
many things since you read his last book, he
has given you a few harder words and longer
sentences, to try your scholarship. Promising
that if you like his third book, he will not
forget you, but soon give you a still newer
one, he signs himself,

UNCLE JOHN.

CONTENTS.

UNCLE JOHN'S THIRD BOOK.

THE FARM-YARD.

THIS is a Farm-yard. Come, good girls
and boys, John will show you all that is in

the Farm-yard.   Look, Rose, at the red Cow;
when the maid milks her you may have a
cup of the nice fresh new milk.

No beast that God gives to man is of more
use to him than the Cow.   The poor man can
live well, if he can keep a good Cow.   Milk
makes a great part of the food of the poor,
and boys and girls like milk more than tea.
Then the cream can be sold to buy bread.
The rich buy the cream from the poor to use
for their tea, and for their cook to make good
things.   The flesh of the Cow is beef, which is
good food.   The thick and strong skin of the
Cow is of great use to make boots and shoes;
the bones are of use for spoons and such
small things, and the horns and the hoofs help
to make glue.

So you must see how much we ought to
thank God for the Cow.

See, the farmers are loading the carts with
the hay which was cut this morning; they will

work all day to get the hay into the large barn you see by the farm-house, so that when summer is over, there will still be plenty of food for the horses, cows, and sheep.

THE NEW BROTHER.

"Come and look here, Mary. I have something to show you that will make you very happy."

"Oh, nurse, what is it?"

"Come and see what I have got in my lap."

"A baby! Oh, nurse, whose baby is it? Where did you get it?"

"It is your little brother, my dear child. God has given it to your mamma, and it is come to live in the nursery with you and me."

"Oh how delightful! What, always to stay here? My little brother! I cannot understand it at all. I shall be too happy."

"Gently, my dear child. You will be very happy I am sure, but not too happy, I hope. Now look at him, and keep quiet at my knee; for your mamma is not well, and you must not make a noise."

"Oh, nurse, let me go and see dear mamma."

"You shall go by-and-by, my dear; but not now. Sit and look at your little brother; and tell me what you think of him."

"Oh, nurse, he is lovely. Only so very tiny, and he keeps his eyes shut so fast."

"He will soon grow bigger; and when his eyes are open, you will see they are pretty bright blue."

"May he have a bit of my cake, nurse? I have such a nice one in the plate that Aunt Jane gave me."

"He cannot eat, my dear child; he has no teeth yet. He will live on milk for a long time. See how feeble he is. His little hands can hold nothing yet; and, if I were to put him on the ground, he would fall down and have no power to move himself."

"Then is he ill, nurse? What makes him so very weak?"

"You were just the same, Mary, when you were first born. And for many months you lay as he does now, a helpless baby on the lap or in the arms. But we took care of you. We carried you while you could not walk, and your dear mamma fed you whilst you could not eat. She taught you to step when you grew stronger, and held you that you might not fall and hurt yourself. At last you could walk, and your mouth was full of pretty white teeth, so that you could eat. You will see how helpless your little brother is; and you may be quite sure that all the pains and care that we take of him were once taken with yourself by your dear mamma and me."

"Well, nurse, it is very strange! I, that now can run and eat so well. It does not seem as

if I ever could have been so tiny and so weak.
You will let me help you to take care of my
little brother, will you not, dear nurse? O, I
shall love him so much. He shall have all
my toys and playthings. And I will do all I
can to make him happy. How good God has
been to give me a little brother."

THE SNOW.

"O ROBERT, dear Robert, come to the window. Only look at the garden and the hills."

"Well, Charles, it is only snow. Did you
never see any before? I thought, at least, that
the summer-house had fallen down; or that
James had been cutting down the birch-tree."

"Well; but what shall we do? You know
we were to have gone on the pond to-day to
slide, and now I am sure we shall not be able
to find our way there."

"We could not slide well with all this snow on the ice, even if we could find our way; and I dare say papa would not like us to try. But we can have just as much fun in another way, now the snow is come; and we shall be able to slide again many times before the winter is over, I have no doubt."

"Well, what can we do?"

"Why, make a snow-man, to be sure, and then pelt him down again with snowballs. And pelt one another, and have all sorts of games with the snow. I am quite glad it is come. Make haste down."

"Oh no, I don't care for that; I want to slide."

"Now, dear Charles, don't be silly. You don't know how happy we shall be, and how warm we shall get. Don't fret for what cannot be helped."

But in vain Robert talked, for Charles was so silly as to sit down and cry, because he

could not enjoy the pleasure **he had** set his
heart upon, and he let Robert go out into the
garden all alone, and sat sobbing at the window. But Robert ran about, and had, as he
said, fine fun. He made **a** large **snow-man,**
and as there was a sharp frost, the snow was
hard and firm. Then he made a high wall of
snow, and pretended his man was a soldier
behind it. And, with a heap of snowballs
by his side, he set to work and cannonaded
the wall till it came down, man and all. But,
as papa told him, his poor soldier had **not**
fair play, because you now **he** could not
return the firing. At last, he was quite hot
and tired with his sport, and came in-doors,
and **there** he found Charles cross and cold.
Cross with himself because **he** had not gone
out to play with Robert, **and** cross even with
everybody **round** him. And cold, **because**
he had sat still by the fire, which is not at
all the best way of warming one's self in the

winter. I am glad to say that he got into a better state of mind at night, when he said his prayers, and he resolved not to be so silly another day.

———

HUMANITY TOWARDS INSECTS.

TURN, turn, thy hasty foot aside,
  Nor crush that helpless worm;
The frame thy scornful thoughts deride,
  From God receiv'd its form.

The common Lord of all that move,
  From whom thy being flow'd,
A portion of his boundless love
  On that poor worm bestow'd

The Sun, the Moon, the Stars HE made
  To all his creatures free;
And spreads o'er earth the grassy blade,
  For worms as well as thee.

Let them enjoy their little day,
Their humble bliss receive ;
Oh ! do not lightly take away
The life thou canst not give.

THE SHIP.

COME with me to the beach, John and Tom,
and we will look at the large Ship now in
sight, for it will soon sail past us. Though it
seems so near to us, it is at least a mile from

us. It sails on the smooth sea, with its white sails spread to the sun, as if no harm could ever come to it. But we know that the wind may rise, and the waves may dash on that strong Ship till it breaks with their weight. Or a storm may drive it to some rough rocks, that may break the fair Ship in pieces, till it is lost in the waves, and all the brave men who now guide it on its way may sink to death.

Let us pray God to watch and spare the Ship and its brave crew, who cross the seas to bring stores for us.

A ship is of great use, for you know there are a great many countries in the world that men wish to see, and a great many of the useful things that are in our houses are brought from distant countries. Tea comes from China; coffee and sugar are brought from the West Indies; rice and cotton from India; oranges and lemons from Spain;

2

apples, plums, and grapes from France; **even**
butter and eggs are brought over from
Ireland in Ships; and thus we obtain many
good things from other nations, and are able
to send them back corn, and coal, and hard-
ware, and cotton goods which we have, in
exchange, which we could not do without
Ships.

HOW TO ENJOY A HOLIDAY.

" How merry you seem, Ralph, over your
work. Do not you get very tired of sitting
here day after day mending old shoes **and**
boots? Every morning when I go by to
school you are hard at work, and at night as
I go home and look in at your window, there
you are stitching or knocking away as busy
as a bee. Don't you long to go out in the
fields and lanes? Oh, if I were a man like

you, I would not stay in-doors this bright summer through. But I would rise with the lark, and be off amongst the cowslips and the blue-bells, or lose myself in the shady woods where the birds are singing so sweetly, and never go to school, or work, or do any thing but amuse myself from morning till night."

"And then, Master Tom, you would not be half so **happy as** I am. For you would not be doing your duty. Do you think you **were** sent into this world for nothing but to amuse yourself? And would it **be** right to think only of your own pleasure? But, even if it were, I do not believe you would find it in idleness. No one can be really happy who is doing wrong. And to waste time cannot be *right.* How do you feel, when you **are** coming home from school at night, when you have been a good boy all day?"

"Well, very happy, Ralph."

"Yes, happier than you do at the end of a whole holiday; do you not?"

"Yes, I think I do; for then I am tired and sorry it is over."

"Ah, Master Tom, depend upon it people are never so happy as when they are doing their duty, even if that duty is hard work, as it must often be in this world. There is always a sort of pleasure mixed up with it that is never found in idleness or wrong-doing. When I sit here in my little room the sun looks in upon me with such a bright ray, it is almost as if he smiled at me. And the linnet in the cage sings me a happy song, and Peter, the little raven, sits and watches how I get on. And the flowers in the window give a pleasant scent. So that I have the sunshine, and birds and flowers, without going from my work. And, if I make haste and can get done in time, I often can patch up an old pair of shoes for a poor neighbor without charge. And that you may be sure is a good plan for ending my day happily. Then on Sundays, those blessed days of rest, I can walk in the fields and enjoy all their beauty with a light heart."

"Well, Ralph, I dare say you are right; and so I will try to do as you do, and get through my day's work cheerfully. For, after all, I should not like to grow up a dunce, as I certainly should if I played about all day instead of going to school. So I will not waste my time talking any more, but run off at once. Only tell me how you made Peter so tame."

"Why, Master Tom, I found him one Sunday afternoon lying in the old churchyard, under the wall. He was very young, and the nest by some accident had fallen down with him in it. He was too young to fly, and I brought him home and fed him with a spoon. He soon grew tame; and now, though he is fully fledged, he will not leave me. I think he even loves me; for you see, Master Tom, I have been a sort of father to him."

"I am sure he ought to love you, Ralph, for taking such good care of him. Now good-bye, I am really going."

"So do, Master Tom, and pray stop in your way home, and tell me whether you have had a happy day. But mind you must work *hard.*"

"So I will, Ralph."

THE LITTLE DOG THAT LOVED HIS MISTRESS.

I HAD once a little dog that I loved very much. He was always with me, and was quite my companion. I used to call him my four-footed friend. He loved me better than any one else in the house, and would not eat his dinner if I was not at home to give it to him. But I did not often leave him behind me, for he was so good and gentle that all my friends were glad to see him. He did not like water, I mean swimming in water, and it was always needful to throw him in when he was to have a bath; for he would not take it of his own accord. But once, when I was out with a party of friends, and some of us got into a boat upon the river, little Elfin was left to run beside us on the bank. But so much was he afraid of losing his dear mistress, that he plunged into the water and came swimming after us. His love for me was stronger than his fear of the water. And, dripping as he was, we were obliged to take him into the boat. I could not be angry with him, for it was so pleasant to be the object of such faithful love. Poor little dog, he is not here now; and sorely do I miss him and his pretty ways. He grew very ill one day. We went for the dog doctor, who did all he could to save him; but it was of no use, for he died at the end of the third day. He lies buried in the garden, under a little fir-tree, and even Baby will not set his tiny foot upon poor "Bow-wow's grave."

WORK.

Do you see this band of negroes working? They are carrying bags of coffee, rice, sugar, and spice upon their heads from the wharf to the great ship which you see lying at the landing. It is hard work to carry such heavy burdens through the heat of the day in Southern climates, yet the negro toils uncomplainingly and patiently. Let us hope that they will have a good meal and a soft bed to rest upon after their day's toil. There is no rest so sweet as that which follows work, when the tired body is refreshed by well-earned labor. The idle and lazy never enjoy this rest. Idleness is well named the parent of all vice.

It is the will of God that no one should waste time in this world. He has said that all must work. Rich and poor, young and old, all have their work to do. The poor man works that he may live: the rich man lives that he may work: the poor man works with his hands, the rich man with his head; but both must work to do God's will.

Your work is to learn well, and with all your heart. To think is to work; to read is to work; to pray is to work; to do the will of God and of those who teach you, is to work. You live for this, and you must not waste one hour of life, or when death is near, you will think with grief on that lost hour.

Think on these things, my child, and learn when you are young, that you may do the will of God in life, and feel peace in death.

THE OTHER NAME FOR REAL POLITENESS.

POLITENESS is a very necessary and valuable accomplishment, or rather I should say quality, and no one should think it beneath him to be polite. But when I speak of its being valuable, I mean real true politeness, **and** not those artificial manners which are taught and learnt as mere matters of outward show; just like those tricks which one can teach to a dog or monkey, and which are very amusing in them, but worse than laughable in a rational creature.

Now I will tell you a story, which will show what I mean by real politeness. And I think we shall find that it is, after all, less an accomplishment than a quality of the mind or heart. For an accomplishment **is** something that we learn, something we acquire; but true politeness springs from the very heart.

Little Sydney was a boy of about eight years old. **He** went to school, and learnt dancing **and** drilling, and **I** know not what besides, in order to teach him manners, or to make him polite. And no boy could make a better bow than Sidney; and as to taking the wall of a lady, dear, dear, he would have run under the very horses' heads in the **street**, rather than think of such a thing.

One day, he was going to school on a dancing afternoon, and he was dressed all in his best, and looking very smart indeed, when he

met a poor beggar woman. She was old and
almost blind, and her clothes were ragged
and dirty. Sidney was not yet perhaps old
enough to have learned, as he ought, to love
the poor for whom Jesus when on earth cared
so greatly; but he surely should have shown
some of his politeness to this poor old woman,
at least so far as to give her the wall. For
though it was not her right, according to the
rules of artificial politeness, yet it is always
our duty to give way to those older or more
afflicted than ourselves. But Sidney's politeness was all outward show, and pushing rude-
ly past the old woman, he almost threw her
down in his eagerness to thrust her from the
wall, against which she was groping her way
along. A few steps more, and he met Mary
Lacey, **a** nice little girl whom everybody
loved, and before whom Sidney was always
very anxious **to** show off his good manners.
Oh, then, how hastily **he** called them all forth,

and with hat off, and foot forward in the very newest style, he took hold of the little lady's hand. As Mary was returning from the errand on which she was bound when she met Sydney, she also came upon the poor old beggar woman, who was waiting to be able to cross the road. "Do let me help you," said Mary: "we can get over nicely now, and if you will put your hand on my shoulder I will lead you the right way."

This was real politeness: it came from the heart, and was not put on for the purpose of display. Mary could not courtesy so gracefully as Sidney could bow, but I think she was more really polite. She had that true politeness of which the Scripture name is Charity, or Love.

BUNKER HILL MONUMENT.

BUNKER HILL MONUMENT.

THIS splendid monument is on Bunker Hill, Charlestown, Mass. It was erected at a great expense to mark the spot where a great battle was fought in the Revolution. Perhaps you have heard your grandfather, or grandmother, tell of the hard times our soldiers had, and how bravely they bore all their sufferings, in order that our country should be free. All American children should love to read and hear about those times, and learn all they can about the great and good Washington. A good young Frenchman named Lafayette came to this country to help us to fight for our liberty. General Washington loved him very much, and so did all our soldiers; and many years after our country was free, he came again to visit it.

On this occasion the first, or corner-stone as it is called, of the Bunker Hill Monument was laid. It was a grand scene. Thousands of people were in the streets and on the ground where the monument now stands. Mr. Webster made the speech, and the ceremonies concluded by all the great multitude singing the grand tune of "Old Hundred."

THE STRAY LAMB.

THE sun was going down slowly into the west, behind a thick curtain of golden and purple clouds, when a little lamb, that had long looked with wandering and restless eyes beyond the fences of his peaceful fold, leaped softly over the wattles, and stopping with a panting heart to listen if his mother bleated to call him back, began to hurry towards a pleasant hill that had long tempted him to go astray. But his mother did not call him. She knew not that he had left her side. She had lain quietly down to sleep, and was dreaming of her little wandering son, who was already far away.

On and on he went, till at last the fold to which he looked back was quite dim in the distance. For the sun was now gone quite out of sight, and the shades of evening were falling like a veil around him. He began to be afraid. It was so still and lonely. He missed the pleasant bleating of his dear companions that was like sweet music as they settled down to sleep.

His mother's side; O! he would have liked to lie down by it now, and rest his little weary feet. And the hill, that looked so tempting when gilded by the light of day, lay black and gloomy before him in the twilight hour.

Poor foolish little lamb, why did you wander from your best friend and your happy fold? All that glitters in the distance is not beautiful, and the path that leads you from

3

your mother and your home cannot **be the** way to happiness.

Now by the side of this hill lay a thick grove of trees, that had often seemed to the little lamb as one of the sweetest play-places that could be found on earth. He had watched the bright birds sporting over its waving green, and had even seen the wild stag couching at its entrance. And he had thought how much happier he should be gambolling about amongst the shady trees than always feeding on the smooth surface of his well-known fold. He forgot that the sun does not always shine; that birds are not forever on the wing; nor stags the only wild creatures in the shady woods.

It was now night, and he had never thought of that, nor where he should rest when absent from his mother's pillow. And he stopped and listened to try and catch some familiar murmur from his home to break the lonely silence round him. But either the fold was too distant, or the sheep were already fast asleep. And as the glow-worms came out upon the dewy grass, they lighted up tears in the eyes of the repentant little lamb.

He trembled, and was afraid to move; for he knew not which way to go, nor where he could find a bed to screen him from the chilly evening air. And there came a sound to his ears that he had never heard before, and yet it thrilled him to the very heart with terror, it was so full of awful meaning. It was the howling of a wolf. And he thought it came nearer as he listened. Then he fell upon the ground in an agony, and had no longer power to run away.

But the good shepherd who took care of the sheep in that happy fold was coming with his faithful dog to find the little truant. He had been to count his sheep and lambs, and one was missing. A tuft of white wool upon the top of the fence had shown him where the restless little lamb had leaped over, and his dog had tracked its wandering feet to the very border of the wood.

Poor little lamb, as it lay and panted on **the** ground, and heard the rustling feet of the good dog come nearer and nearer, it gave itself up for lost; for it thought the wolf must be close **at** hand. But the dog had found it first, and **it soon** lay nestling in the shepherd's bosom, almost too happy that it was safe once more.

The wolf's voice was heard further and further in the distance as the little lamb was carried back to its quiet fold; and, oh! how blessed a refuge did its fences now seem to enclose. No more a prison, as it had once seemed, but a very nest of peace.

His mother looked up in wonder, as he was **laid** down beside her by the good shepherd; **but** she never knew how nearly she had lost him forever. Scarcely would **he** ever quit her from that hour, and if his eyes by chance turned towards the hill and wood that had been so all but fatal to him, with what a thrill of ecstacy would he think of his present safety, and how far more beautiful was the happy fold than all that lay beyond it.

Dear little children, you who are still in the house of your father and your mother, think of it as the peaceful fold, where like little lambs you may dwell in safety.

Do not break the rules that are set around like fences to enclose you more securely: nor fancy that forbidden ways must lead to new pleasures. It has never yet been so, and never will it be. Only in the fold is there such safety and such peace; for beyond it there are dangers and troubles of which you little dream, and there is not always a kind hand near to bring home little wandering lambs in safety.

TO A LADY-BIRD.

"LADY-BIRD! Lady-bird! fly away home,"
 The field-mouse has gone to her nest,
The daisies have shut up their sleepy red eyes,
 And the bees and the birds are at rest.

"Lady-bird! Lady-bird! fly away home,"—
 The glow-worm is lighting her lamp,
The dew's falling fast, and **your** fine speckled
  wings
 Will flag with the close-clinging damp.

"Lady-bird! Lady-bird! fly away home,"—
 Good luck if you reach it at last,
The owl's come abroad, and the bat's on the
  roam,
 Sharp set from their Ramagan fast.

"**Lady-bird**! **Lady-**bird! **fly away** home,"—
 The fairy-bells tinkle afar,

Make haste, or they'll catch ye and harness ye
    fast.
    With a cobweb to Oberon's car.

"Lady-bird! Lady-bird! fly away home,"—
    But as all serious people do, first
Clear your conscience, and settle your world-
    ly affairs,
    And so be prepar'd for the worst.

"Lady-bird! Lady-bird!" make a short shrift,
    Here's a hair-shirted Palmer hard by,
And here's lawyer Earwig to draw up your
    will,
    And we'll witness it, Death-moth and I.

"Lady-bird! Lady-bird!" don't make a fuss,—
    You've mighty small matters to give,
Your coral and jet, and . . . there, there . . .
    you can tack
    A codicil on if you live.

"Lady-bird! Lady-bird!" fly away now,—
　　To your house in the old willow-tree,
Where your children, so dear, have invited
　　　the ant,
　　And a few cozy neighbors to tea.

"Lady-bird! Lady-bird! fly away home,"—
　　And if not gobbled up by the way,
Nor yoked by the fairies to Oberon's car,
　　You're in luck—and that's all I've to say.

THE BEAVER.

THE Beaver is only found in the cold regions of the North of Asia; and in America, where immense numbers are caught, for the sake of their skins, which are of value in making hats.

In summer a number of these active little creatures meet on the banks of a still pool or narrow river, to build their winter houses. They begin by damming the water, by gnawing down a tree with their sharp teeth, and letting it fall across; this bar they make complete with short sticks woven. Then they build their houses of sticks and stones, on piles, at the edge of the stream, and plaster them within and without with mud, by means of their flat, long tail. So neat, well made, and smooth are these houses, that you might fancy them the work of man. In these houses they store food for winter; in summer they live on berries, herbs, and fruits.

THE VALUE OF TRUTH.

"Who broke this window, children?" said a poor woman, as she ran hastily out of her cottage on hearing a pain of glass smash.

There were a great many **boys** and girls playing in the road close by, and when they **saw** the woman come out they all began loud-**ly to** declare that they had none of them done it. "We none of us did it; it was not any of us. You must have thrown something against it yourself in the house."

All, except one little boy who looked very pale and frightened; but he went towards the angry woman and said, "I did it. I am very sorry, it was broken by a stick which sprung suddenly out of my hand."

"O, you did it, did you," said the woman; "and pray can you pay for **it**?"

"No," said the little boy; "**I** have no money."

"Of course you have not," answered the woman angrily; "and so I shall just give you this to make you remember to be more careful another time." And seizing the poor child, she struck him several hard blows. He did not cry, however; and, when she had gone back into her cottage, the other children gathered round him.

"How could you be so silly, Arthur? We all said we did not do it; and if you had not gone and told her yourself, she would never have known any thing about it."

"But I did do it," said Arthur.

"Yes; but it was not you any more than James, for he was pulling your hand, and that was what made the stick fly out of it."

"Well, there was no need to tell of James," answered Arthur; "it was my stick."

"Well," cried James, "I am very glad I did not tell of myself, to get beaten as you did. Are not you very sorry now that you told?"

"No, for if **I** had said I did not do it, I should have told **a** lie. And if I had been silent while all of you were saying it **was** none of us, that would **have** been *almost* if not *quite* as wrong."

The other children laughed at Arthur; and they went further away from the cottage and began to play again.

You will see by this story that Arthur loved the truth, and feared a lie. He knew that God hates liars; and he **was** never **half** so much afraid of any punishment that might come upon him for speaking the truth, as he was of incurring the anger of God by telling a lie. He was well taught; and he knew, that though by saying he had done something or other for which he was sure to be punished, **he** might **get** even a painful beating, yet that the pain of those blows would soon pass away; whilst if he escaped them by telling a lie, it would be written in God's book of remembrance and stand there against him. Besides, even without bringing this awful thought into his mind, he thought it was cowardly to tell a lie, and even that, in the end, those who always spoke the truth got on better in this world ; and the course of his after-life made him feel this still more strongly.

At school he was known and thoroughly trusted by his master, who, if there was any doubt about any thing that happened amongst the boys, always called Arthur up to tell him exactly the facts of the case; for then he said he should know just what was the matter and who was to blame. And when he left school, and was placed in a counting-house, he was so truthful and exact that the greatest dependence was placed upon him, and he rapidly rose in his employer's confidence. One day there were some mistakes in one of the books which threw all the accounts into disorder. The principal was very much displeased, and began inquiring to see if he could find out how the original mistake had happened, and by whom it was made. Arthur set to work diligently to help him, and at last found that he had made a blunder in some calculation, which had afterwards been copied by another clerk, and so had gone on through the different books without being discovered. Now it would have been easy enough to let the blame rest on the young man who had copied it; for the original paper was in Arthur's own possession, and he could have concealed it. But without allowing such a thought to cross his mind, he ran directly and went nobly to his employer, and confessed his error with much regret. The gentleman looked up with a cleared brow at Arthur, and said, " All the trouble this has caused me is nothing now I have the satisfaction of finding such an honorable man in my employment. My confidence in you will be indeed increased instead of lessened by this event.

Arthur bowed and his heart was full; but what he had done was little in his own eyes; for he had, when young, acquired so strictly the *habit* of always telling the truth that it never, now he was a man, occurred to him to do otherwise. And this, dear children, is one great advantage of always being careful to speak the exact truth; the habit will become so natural to you, that you will soon never think of doing any thing else.

Arthur continued for many years in the same house, and at last was made a partner by his grateful master. And, when he was raised to this dignity, he tried to use all his influence over the clerks they employed to induce them to be as careful as himself; for, he would often say, "You will not have half so much trouble if you tell me the truth at once: for, I shall be sure to inquire very closely into the matter if I think you deceive me, and you will have to make up ever so many tales to bear out what you now say. It **is** unworthy of a man, or even a child, and most sinful before God, to hide **the** truth by a lie."

THE HAPPY RABBIT.

JOHN and Kitty have a pretty white rabbit. It has long drooping ears, and bright sparkling eyes. John himself helped to make its house at the side of the stable; and he took care that it should have plenty of room to run about in. For rabbits are wild active creatures, and love liberty dearly. If you have ever seen them as I have often, frisking about on a sunny down, now darting over the short turf and then popping into their holes—you will know at once how hard it must be for a rabbit to be shut up **in a** small den, where he has but just room enough to turn round, and where the only peep of daylight he gets is through two or three little bars.

John and Kitty know well what rabbits love, and though their pretty pet was never at liberty, for he was not a wild rabbit, yet they try all they can to give him those enjoyments which are natural to him. So the hutch is made very roomy and large. And two or three times a day, in fine weather, he is taken out of his house and allowed to run about a paved yard, to stretch his legs and take the air. And he is well fed with wild parsley and bran, and lettuce leaves, and all sorts of things that rabbits love. And he well repays this care by growing very fat and strong, and by loving his little master and mistress with all his bunny heart. When he hears their steps in the yard, he runs directly to the nice large barred window John made for him that he might get plenty of light, and puts his white nose out as far he can to welcome them.

4

Once they took him out of his house, and carried him into a field close by, that he might nibble some fresh clover that was blowing there. But, once in the open country, bunny's natural instinct came upon him, and he set off, racing across the field, so fast that John and Kitty were in despair, and feared they had lost him entirely. But running as fast as they could in the direction he had taken, they overtook him at last, digging with all his might in the soft earth under a hedge. He had already burrowed quite a a hole, by scraping the earth up with **his** fore paws and throwing it out beyond his hind legs. He **was so** busily at work, making himself **a** home I suppose, that he did not notice John and Kitty, who pounced delighted upon their little runaway, and carried him home. **And** he never **was** allowed to have a scamper in the field again, so much had he frightened his little friends.

ESQUIMAUX AND THEIR HUTS.

THE Esquimaux inhabit the extreme northern part of North America, commonly called the
Arctic Regions.   It is very cold indeed where
they live, a great deal colder than any little
boy or girl who reads this can imagine.   They

live in huts made of ice and snow. These huts are sometimes round, a layer of stones being placed on a bank of snow, then their paddles, tent-poles, pieces of whalebone, are added, and when they can get them, birch-twigs for beds. A round piece of ice covers the top. They make a kind of tunnel by which they enter and leave the hut, creeping in and out. The hut not having any opening for fresh air becomes very hot, and the water melting from the snow inside makes them very wet. They crowd a great many persons into very small space. The Esquimaux live entirely by hunting and fishing, as it is too cold for any thing to grow there. Their clothes are made of skins of beasts and birds, and their spears and arrows of bones of **fishes**. Their canoes are very light and small, mostly made of whalebone. They are a very dirty, ignorant people, but in many instances have shown themselves very kind-hearted **to** the different persons who have been lost on their coasts.

_____

THE CONTRARY BOY.

Do you know what a contrary boy is? I will tell you. He is one who is never satisfied with what he has, but always wants something different. If I were to say to you, "Come, James, and see what a pretty picture I have got here;" and you should say, "No, I don't want a picture, you said you would bring me a pretty book,"—that would be being *contrary*. If your father should bring you home a little cart to draw about the room, and you should say, "I don't want a cart, I don't like carts, I want a horse and whip, like William's," that would be very contrary.

Now I knew a little boy once, who was very unhappy a great deal of his time because he would not be pleased with the playthings he had, but always wanted another kind, or something else. This little boy had a very kind father and mother, who loved him very much, and who tried to make him happy. They bought him good clothes to wear; they gave him good things to eat, whenever he was hungry, and they bought him a great many pretty playthings. But though they were so very kind, this boy was sometimes so naughty as to cry when they gave him a new plaything, because he had wanted a cart, or a whip, perhaps, instead of a pretty wooden box of blocks. If they had bought him either of these, he would have wanted the blocks or something else. Nobody liked to give Charles any playthings, or sugar-plums, or any thing else, because they did not make him happy; and they did not make him happy because he would not be pleased, but always thought of something else which he fancied he would rather have.

One day Charles's mother came into the room where he was playing, and said, "Charles, your little brother William is going to walk with Susan; would you like to go too?"

"Yes," said he, "but I shall want to wear my new cap."

"But I told you the other day," said his mother, "that you could not wear it for a whole week again, because you threw it upon the floor when you came in yesterday, instead of hanging it on its nail."

"Then I don't want to go," said Charles.

"Very well," said his mother; and calling to Susan, she told her she need not to wait any longer.

"But I *shall* want to go," said Charles, beginning to cry.

"You must not go now," said his mother, "for you said you did not want to go, just because you felt contrary, and out of humor."

His mother then sat down to work.

Charles, finding it was useless to cry, dried his tears, and began throwing his playthings about the room.

"Don't do so," said his mother; "you will break that pretty box, and your white **cards**, with the pretty colored letters, will get soiled, and not fit to be used."

"I **don't** care if they do," said Charles; "it is not a pretty box, and I don't like the cards."

His mother rose, took away all his playthings, and left him sitting upon the floor, with nothing to do. As she took no notice of his cross looks, he presently went to the window, and **stood on a** little stool, looking to see the horses and carriages passing, and soon **he** began to feel good-humored again.

"Oh! mother," said he, "there are two beautiful little dogs in the street, and a little boy running after them. Oh! how I should like a little dog. Mother, will you buy me one ?" and he ran to his mother, and looked up in her face.

" What would you do with a dog, "said his mother " if you had one ?"

" Oh ! I should play with him ; I would put some things in my cart, and tie the dog to it, and let him draw it to market, just like the dog in William's picture. "

" But I am afraid," said his mother, " that if your father should buy **you** a dog, you would sometimes get out of humor with him, and then you would say it was an ugly dog, and you did not want it any more."

" No I would not," said Charles ; " **I should** always love my little dog."

" So you said, if I would buy you a new cap, you would be a good boy, and never give me any trouble about it ; but yesterday you forgot your promise, and did not put it in its place : and to-day you have made me very unhappy by your bad temper. And you have displeased God too, for he was looking directly into your heart when you said you did not want to go with Susan, and saw that you were saying what was not true."

" But I will remember next time, if you will only get me a little dog."

Just then William came into the room with a large piece of cake in his hand, which a lady had given him. He went up to his brother, and breaking it into two pieces, offered him one of them.

" No, I want the other piece," said Charles.

" But I can't give it to you," said William ; " I want it myself."

" Then I won't have any," said Charles, impatiently.

" Keep all the cake yourself, William," said his mother; " Charles must not have any, because he is not a good boy."

" But I do want some," said Charles, beginning to cry very loud. Then his mother went to the door, and calling Susan, told her to take Charles into the other room, and keep him there until he was perfectly good-humored. So you see Charles lost a pleasant walk and a nice piece of cake, and after all had to be sent away from his kind mother, just because he would be a contrary boy. Do you think he was happy?

In the afternoon, Charles and his brothers and sisters went to play in the meadows. It was a beautiful day, for the sun shone very splendidly, and the birds were singing merrily. After having amused themselves for some time, so that they began to feel tired, they sat down to rest under the shade of an over-hanging tree.

"Here is a beautiful flower, Susan," said Charles; "it is prettier *by far*, than any which you have gathered; would you not like to have it? if you would, I will give it you.

Here, Susan, take it—I know it will please you."

"Thank you, my dear brother," replied his sister; "it really is very handsome, and I am sure it will be a great addition to my nose-gay."

She then stretched out **her** arm for the purpose of taking it—but just as she had hold of it, the contrary boy drew back his hand with great force, saying, "No, I want it myself;" by which means the flower was destroyed.

The next day, as these two little boys were playing in the yard, they looked up and saw a carriage, drawn by two large white horses, stop at the door. It was their aunt's. She had brought her little son and daughter, named James and Mary, to spend the afternoon with their cousins, and all looked as happy as if they were expecting to have a rare good time; **and so** they **were.**

Their aunt went into the house, and the children played together out in the yard. When they were tired of that, they went into the mowing field, where the hay was spread to dry, and began to throw it upon each other. This they enjoyed very much, till Charles began to cry, and said they should not throw the hay upon him. He wanted to pelt the others, but was not willing to have them pelt him. So this contrary boy spoiled the whole play, and he cried so loud that his mother had to call him into the house. When he was gone, James laid down in the hay, and told his sister and cousin to cover him up in it. When he was hidden entirely, so that they could not see him, he jumped up suddenly, and ran to catch them, with an armful of hay, to pay them for treating him so. They laughed very loud, and were very happy, now they had no one to disturb them with crying. They were soon called in to tea.

Charles had not been very well in the morning, and his mother was afraid to give him as many strawberries in his milk as the rest. So Charles began to cry, and said he would not have any. His mother then sent him out of the room, and did not allow him to return until his cousins had gone.

You see how many pleasant things he lost by being so contrary. His mother said she could not buy him a dog until he had learned to be a good boy. His cousins said they did not want to go see and him again, for he spoiled their play; and when his mother went to see his aunt, she took William, but left Charles at home. She said she could not take him with her until he was willing to do as others wished to have him, and not always cry to have his own way. By-and-by Charles learned that it was better to be pleasant at all times, and not get out of humor when things did not exactly suit him; and then everybody loved him, for he was a good little boy in every other respect.

—

THE CAMEL.

THE CAMEL AT HOME.

"O, MAMMA, I saw a camel go by. A real, large, live camel. A man led it by a rope."

"Poor thing! I am very sorry for it, my dear."

" Why, mamma ? "

" Because, my dear, the camel is the native of a warmer land than ours, and it was not meant by God to be led about on rough and stony roads. Its feet are soft and spongy, and only fitted for the yielding sands of its own country."

"Then I am sorry for it too, mamma; very sorry. I did not know it was cruel. Where does the camel come from, mamma ? "

" Arabia is its native home, my dear. There it is used by the Arabs as a beast of burden, and will carry heavy loads for a great distance. It is taught to kneel down at the word of command, in order that it may be more easily laden. And it is much more useful than a horse could be in that burning land, where water is very scarce; because it has cells or bags within its stomach, which will retain the water it drinks for many days, so that it does not grow thirsty again as long as this supply lasts. And it can smell so keenly, that if there is a fountain two miles off it will find it out, thus often saving the lives of whole cara- vans. A caravan is a company of people, and their horses and camels, travelling over the sands. It is usual to go in large parties, for the dangers of the wide deserts are very great. The camel's nostrils are so formed, that it can close them if it likes. And this is because sometimes a whirlwind raises and drives the sand, so as almost to suffocate those who meet it. So you see, dear, how good God has been in fitting the camel for the land it inhabits, and how wrong it must be to bring it away, and drag it about the streets of a country where every thing is so different that it must often suffer sadly."

5

LITTLE JESSIE AND HER NEW SHILLING.

LITTLE Jessie **was** eight years old. She
could read and spell very nicely, and she
loved a pretty book dearly. And she could
work far more neatly than many an older child,
because she took pains, and was more careful
to work *well* than quickly. One day she had
finished a new pillow-case. She had made it
all herself. She had even sewn on the strings
and marked it. And her mamma was pleased.
So much pleased with her dear little girl that
she said, " You have taken so much pains to do
this work well, dear Jessie, that I should like
to give you something as a reward. Here is
a bright new shilling for you. And after din-
ner you shall go down to the shop in the village, and buy what you like with it." Jessie
kissed her dear mamma, and her eyes shone
with joy. **But it** was more because she had
pleased her mother than for the sake of the

shilling, and she said, "Dear mamma, do not give me the money. I do not want to be paid for my work. You do not know how happy I am to do any thing for you." "I know that, my love," said her mamma, "and I do not give you this as payment for your work, for I know *that* was an act of love; but I like to show you how much I am pleased with you. So take the shilling, my dear child, and buy something to keep for my sake." Then Jessie took the pretty new shilling, and her eyes filled with tears, she was so happy. When she read a chapter in the Bible that morning, as she always did every day after her lessons were over, she came to that text, "Do unto others as you would they should do unto you." And her mamma talked to her about it for a little while. Then Jessie went to play in the garden, and after dinner she put on her bonnet and jacket to go down to the village shop. She was always trusted to go there by herself, **for it was** not far, and on the same side of the way as her mamma's house, so **that** she had not to cross the road. She had quite made up her mind what she would buy with her shilling. For in the window of the village shop had long stood open a very charming story book full of pictures and pretty tales. And "one shilling" was written just above it. So on this book Jessie set her heart, and bounding merrily down the stairs, and only stopping to give one kiss to her dear mamma, she was soon in the village street, on her way to spend the money. She had not gone far, **when** she met little Sally James, crying very bitterly. Sally was about Jessie's age, and the child of very poor and very sickly parents, who had often not food enough to give their hungry little girl. **Her** face looked sad indeed by Jessie's happy one, nor was there any need to ask the reason of her tears. **A** brown loaf was in her little apron, which she had just been to fetch from the shop to which Jessie was going. And a jug of milk had been in her hand. But, alas! poor little girl, her shoes were old, and wanted mending sadly. One of them had caught in a rough flint stone, and the jerk had thrown her down. The milk was spilt and the jug broken to pieces. The milk was all they had for supper with the brown loaf, as she sobbingly told Jessie; and the jug, it was the only one in the house. Jessie had often been with her mamma to visit the poor in their own homes. And she had learned to feel for their sorrows and sufferings. So she saw at once how real a trial little Sally's was, and that the loss of the milk and the jug was a very different thing to Sally to what it would have been in her own case. For if she had met with an accident of the same sort, more milk could have been bought, and there were plenty of jugs to make up the loss of the broken one. But Jessie's kind little heart saw

at once the poor family going to bed without
any thing to soften the coarse bread which
was their only food, and the sad face of the
anxious mother when she found their only jug
was broken. And the blessed text in her
morning's reading came into Jessie's mind, "Do
unto others **as** you would they should do unto you." And with a bright and happy smile
she drew the shining shilling from her little
purse, and said, "Do not cry, Sally; see, you
shall have this pretty new shilling, and we will
go back to the shop and buy a new jug, and
you shall get some more milk." "**Oh,** miss!"
was all that little Sally could reply. The joy
seemed too much after her great sorrow. But
the tears were soon dried up, and the two **lit**
tle girls went together to the shop, and for
sixpence they bought a strong useful jug.
Twopence more filled it with milk, and there
was still fourpence left, which Jessie thought
would be quite enough to pay for mending lit-

tle Sally's ragged shoes. I do not know which little girl was the happiest as they left the shop, but I think Jessie, for we know it is more blessed to give than to receive. And if for a moment, as she passed the window on her way home, the sight of the pretty book cast a shadow on her brow, her heart was filled with a deep peace as she rested her face on her mamma's shoulder, threw her arms round her neck, and told her how she had spent her new shilling.

THE OLD WOMAN BY THE WOOD.

THE OLD WOMAN'S COTTAGE.

THERE was once an old woman who lived
in a cottage close by a wood. The shadow
of some of the nearest trees fell upon the
thatch on sunny days, so that it was almost
as if she lived in the wood itself. Many people thought she must have been very lonely,

for there was no house near her by a mile or
two. But she was far happier than if she had
been dwelling in a crowded street, where
friends and neighbors would have been ever at
her door; for she loved the works of God. And
here, in the shelter of the wood, she could enjoy them with an undisturbed heart. The
birds seemed to her as cheerful friends, and
the flowers were far more beautiful than any
of the treasures man has made. In the night,
the sweet voice of the nightingale kept her
from feeling solitary. And when winter
came, and the trees were bare and the birds
silent, she scattered food for them around her
door, and often tempted them within the
threshold. Even the shy little squirrel, that
jumped out of sight if any other foot came by
its nest, would come shyly from the tree to
watch the old woman scattering corn for its
food.

HOW TO BE GOOD.

" Papa," said Harry, " I mean to be a very good boy all day, to-day. I don't mean to do any thing naughty at all."

"I am very glad to hear it, my boy," said papa, as he went out at the hall door, and left Harry standing on the stone steps.

It was a holiday, and Harry felt so full of spirits, he thought he could do any thing. First he raced round the garden till he was quite out of breath, and then he went to feed his rabbits, and look at Rover in his kennel.

While he was out in the yard, his little sister came running to him. " O, Harry, mamma says you have left all your bricks upon the carpet in the breakfast-room, and you must come and clear them away at once."

" I can't, Jenny: I want to feed the rabbits; they have nothing to eat. Tell mamma I will come presently."

"But mamma said you were to come this very moment, because Ann wants to clean the room."

"I must feed the rabbits now I am here," said Harry. "It won't take me long. I will come the very moment I have done."

So Jenny went back to the house, and Harry began to feed his rabbits. And he found they had been gnawing the hutch-doors, so that one of the leathern hinges had given way. And he was afraid they would get out if he did not mend it. So he fetched his tool-box and set to work. But it was a long job, and more than an hour passed away before he got to the breakfast-room. There all was in disorder. Chairs piled upon one another. The window-curtains all looped up out of the way, and Ann sweeping in such clouds of dust that Harry would gladly have made his escape if he had not felt rather anxious about the fate of his bricks.

"Where are my bricks, Ann? They were all on the carpet."

"I do not know, Master Harry. I have not seen them."

"Not seen them, Ann! You *must* have seen them; for I am sure they were there."

"Well, I can't tell," said Ann. "And now you really must get out of my way, for I am too busy to stand looking for bricks."

"But I want my bricks," said Harry. "And you must tell me this moment where you have put them. I will have them."

Ann's only reply was to take hold of Harry's hand and lead him out of the room; when she shut the door, and again went on with her work. Harry was very angry, and began making such a noise at the closed door that his mamma came down stairs to see what was the matter.

"It is that tiresome Ann, mamma. You know she is always so cross, and now she will not tell me where she has put my bricks, and has turned me out of the room. But I will go in again."

"Harry, Harry," said his mamma, "how can you be so naughty. Did you not come and clear away your bricks, as I told you, an hour ago?"

"I came as soon as I had fed the rabbits, mamma."

"But I told you to come at once. You were not obedient, Harry; and now you must go to your own room for a quarter of an hour. You know I never allow you to disobey me."

So Harry went up stairs, crying and scolding. But at the end of a quarter of an hour he came out, looking brighter, and running to his mamma, he asked her to forgive him.

Little Jenny, who was in the room, said, "Harry, do come and help me to make this card-house. I cannot make the cards stand up at all."

"No, Jenny, I cannot," said Harry. "I have been shut up, now I don't know how long; and all the morning will be gone before I have had any play. Besides, I must find my bricks."

"They are all safe, Harry. I put them away for you," said his little sister. "I put them all in the box, for fear they should get lost."

Harry looked a little ashamed, and thanked his sister; but still he did not offer to help her with the cards, but went down again to the garden. There he lashed the trees and flowers with his new whip, till **he** had broken off the head of a fine lily that his papa **val-**ued very much. And, after that, he went down to the pond, and threw stones in the water till his clothes were splashed all over with mud. He was reproved again when he came in to dinner; and all the afternoon he was in mischief of some sort, so that when his papa came home at night there was a sad account to lay before him.

He sent for Harry to his own room. "Well, Harry, how did you get on to-day? I thought you were to be a very good boy. And I hear of rudeness to the servants, disobedience to your mamma, and so much mischief of one kind or another, that I really do not know what to think of you."

Harry burst into tears. "Yes, papa, I have been very unhappy all day. Every thing has gone wrong with me. And I meant to be so good."

"Yes, my poor boy, I know you did. Tell me, did you say your prayers this morning?"

"No, papa, I am afraid I forgot them. I was rather late, and did not like to stay up stairs any longer to say them."

"Ah, Harry, that is the secret of the unhappy day and all the mischief. You have been trying in your own strength, and have not asked help of God, who alone can give it. Do not you know that of yourself you can do no good thing; but that with God's grace, which is the reward of prayer, you can do all?"

"Yes, papa."

"Then go, my dear child, and pray to God to forgive you. Tell Him how you have forgotten Him through this day, but that you are sorry from your very heart, and ask Him to strengthen you to do better to-morrow."

Then Harry knelt down for his papa's blessing; and going up quietly to his own little room, he tried to pour forth his whole heart to his Father in Heaven.

STROLL ON THE SEA SHORE.

"Now, dear mamma," said Harry, as his mother came from the door of the bathing machine, "will you dress very quickly and take the long walk on the shore that you promised me."

6

"Yes, Harry—you are **already dressed, I see.**"

It was a very impatient Harry, who walked up and down on the beach, waiting for his mother to come to him; but at last when he was almost tempted to think **she** never would come, **she** called to him, and taking his hand, led him, away from the merry groups of bathers, to a quieter part of the beach.

As soon as he was free to run about, Harry began to search for sea treasures to add to his pretty marine store, which he had collected the previous summer. His mother tried to read, seating herself in a pretty grotto, a few **steps** from Harry; but his frequent calls for **her** soon made her put **her book** aside to join **her** little boy and share his pleasure.

As soon as **he saw** that she was ready for a **talk** he sprang to meet her, crying: "O, I have found such a pretty thing. Do look at it. What can it be?"

"It is a star-fish. See, it is just like a star. Put it into the water again. It has been left on the sands by the ebbing tide, and perhaps it will die if we leave it here; or some cruel boy may find it and hurt it. Take it gently up, with some sand under it, on your little wooden spade. There, now you have got it very nicely. And you can put it in here, where the cliffs have formed a little pond. Now it moves. It sinks down into the sands. Now it is gone quite under them."

"O, mamma, I should have liked to keep it so much. I never saw such a pretty thing before."

"I am sure you would not have liked to make it unhappy, my darling. And it would soon have died a painful death if you had kept it.

"Why, mamma?"

"Because, dear, it is a sea-animal, and is made to live in salt water. It could no more live on land than you could in the sea."

"No; I should not like to hurt it, mamma."

"There is a sea-nettle. Is not that a curious thing?"

"Yes, mamma. What is that? It looks like jelly."

"That is an animal too, though one of those wonderful creatures that are almost as much like a plant as a living thing. Do not touch it, for they are said to make the hands of those that touch them tingle. Have you ever seen a sea-anemone amongst the rocks, when out walking?"

"No, mamma; what is it like?"

"Come with me along this rocky ledge, and I dare say we shall find some. There, look down in the water. There are numbers of them. Purple, pink, and green. Are they not beautiful?"

"They are indeed, mamma; just like flowers. And I can see them open and shut themselves up while I watch them. Do they sting?"

"I think not; but you had better not touch them."

"Shall we look for shells? O, mamma, look at the sky! What a lovely color. And just where the sun is going down the clouds are so bright, they make my eyes quite ache to look at them."

"The sky often looks so at sunset by the sea. Look at that white sail in the distance. But the tide is coming in, we must not go further amongst the rocks for fear we should not be able to get back again. Let us keep near the bathing-machines."

HOW TO MAKE A KITE.

A CHINESE KITE.

THERE is scarcely any plaything that a boy can have that is so useful to him as a kite. I will tell you why. He must be ingenious to contrive it; industrious to make it; active to fly it; patient to hold it; and obliging to lend it. So you see that to be a good boy with a good kite requires several virtues—ingenuity, industry, activity, patience, and an obliging disposition.

Kites afford excellent amusement both in making and flying them. Those that are bought at shops are poor things, and it is much better for boys to make their own. To do this, procure first a lath four feet long, an inch wide, and a quarter of an inch thick. The bender (or shoulders of the Chinese kite) must be a cane or hoop planed thin at the edges, and should be as long as the lath. Tie a piece of string to each end of the bender, leaving it long enough to stretch to the end of the lath, when the other end is pressed to the centre of the bender, notching the lath to keep the string in place. Now stretch another string from one end of the bender across to the other, and your frame is made. The best thing to cover it with is thin glazed calico, as it may be put on all in one piece. If paper is used, the sheets must first be pasted together with the edges lapping over each other about half an inch. Lay the frame on the calico or paper, cut it out to the shape, leaving an inch to be turned over and pasted to the frame. Some small pieces must then be pasted over the lath and the strings at the back to keep it secure in the middle. Two holes must be made in the lath at each end, and a piece of strong string stretched across. In the centre of this string is tied the string used to fly the kite. Care must be taken to tie it in the right place; if it be too low, the kite will turn round and round in the air—if too high, it will plunge about and pitch. A little experience will soon teach the proper place to fasten it. The tail should be at least ten times as long as the kite. It is much better not to have slips of paper tied into it, but only a *bob* at the end; that is, a large tassel made of paper cut into fringes, and sufficiently heavy to keep the kite in its true position in the air. Tails made with slips are nearly always troublesome from getting entangled; and as the wind shakes them more than it does a plain string, the kite is not so easily balanced.

When the kite is flying you may send up a *messenger*, which is a round piece of paper, or card-board with a hole in the middle; this is put on the string, and the wind soon carries it up to the kite.

A hollow tube of paste-board, with four little sails attached, forms another kind of messenger. The sails are to be made of colored paper, similar to the little wind-mills often sold in the streets. When the tube is placed on the string, the wind acting on the sails, causes the messenger to rotate or spin round; and this, as it ascends, forms a very pretty object.

THE USE OF A NEEDLE.

FANNY JAMES did not love needle-work.
She thought it tiresome, and it made her finger sore. She liked playing on the piano or
dancing better. And certainly this is a more
pleasant way of spending one's time than sew-
ing. But still every girl ought to know how
to work; and I do not see why boys should
not learn too, at least so far as to be able to
hem a handkerchief or mend a stocking, for
they are very often sadly in want of such
knowledge after they **are** grown up. However, everybody does not think as I do on this
subject, and it is not to our present purpose
to say any more about it. All are agreed that
girls should learn. But Fanny always said,
"Mamma, there is no occasion. Bridget the
nurse does all my mending for me, and you
do not know how I dislike work."

Her mamma was in poor health, and did

not see after any thing very much herself; so Fanny was left to do as she liked, and she grew up without so much as knowing how to make a button-hole. Now, when she was about eighteen, her papa and mamma both died rather suddenly, and in settling all their affairs it was found that there was nothing left for Fanny to live upon: so she was obliged to do what she could to earn her own bread: and a kind lady, who had known her father and mother, offered to take her as a companion, to help her in different ways in the house, as she was rather lame. Fanny felt very grateful for this; and, when her first bitter grief for the loss of her best and dearest friends had a little passed away, she began to feel very happy with Mrs. Stone. But so soon as she was well enough to be employed, she found to her great dismay that needle-work was almost the chief thing that would be required of her after the morning hours. For Mrs.

Stone worked a great deal for the poor and made clothes for them, and she wanted Fanny to sit and help her for the greater part of the day. Then it was that poor Fanny found the folly of her former conduct.

She was now in such circumstances that she did not object to work, as she did when a child; but would gladly have done whatever was required of her. But she did not know how, and being ashamed to tell Mrs. Stone of her childish folly, many and sad were the mistakes she made. One day a pair of sheets were found sewn together like a great pillow-case; and though, as Mrs. Stone said, laughing good humoredly, "Such a plan might save the trouble of tucking up the bed; yet, as it was not the usual way of doing such things, Fanny really must undo her work." She made such sad blunders, that at last Mrs. Stone was obliged to part with her; for she wanted some one who could help her in her deeds of charity, and not hinder them by wasting time and materials. Truly sorry was Fanny to go, and much trouble she had in finding any one willing to take so useless a person. At last she got a situation as nurse to an old lady, who was very ill and very fretful, and who wanted waiting upon every moment of the day. This was very hard work for poor Fanny, but she tried to take it as a wholesome punishment for her folly: yet often she could not help saying to herself, " Oh, if I had but taken pains to learn to work whilst I was at school, I might still have been with that dear Mrs. Stone."

THE MOUSE WHO WANTED TO SEE THE WORLD.

THE OAK TREE.

THERE was once a little brown mouse who
lived in an old oak tree, close to the root.
The tree stood upon a high hill, and from her
nest the mouse could look out over broad

fields, and far away could see a faint line like silver, which was the sea shore. In the summer the large green leaves of the tree made a cool pleasant shade for the mouse's nest, and in the winter she crept far down to the root, curled herself up, and slept safely, sheltered by the strong tree from every wind or storm. It was the grandest tree for a home, and her nest was the very prettiest and the softest that could be thought of. But the little mouse grew tired of the old oak tree, and wanted to see the world. So one day, when the pretty blue-bells were ringing merrily all around her tree, and the morning sun shone brightly in the cloudless sky, away she went for change of air and scene, as she said to herself. Ah, silly little mouse! There is not a mossy nest under every tree in the wide world, and the summer sun does not always shine.

On she went and very much tired she got,

and after all she felt rather disappointed; for there was nothing but trees, and blue-bells, and clear skies, and she wanted change. And change came *too soon*. The sun began to set, **and** the skies grew dark and gloomy, and at last the lightning and thunder and rain came on all around her. And there were no more blue-bells or green trees, for she was out upon a bare common. O, then, how earnestly the little mouse lamented her folly, and how bitterly she sighed after her mossy hole in the old oak tree.

She tried to run back, but her little feet got clogged with mud, for the rain poured heavily. And all night long she wandered about, seeking in vain for shelter. And early in the morning she was seen by **a** shepherd-boy who had come out betimes **to** work, and he carried her home and shut her up in a dismal box with only four little bars to peep through at the light of day; and dry brown

bread and bad apples were all she got to eat,
instead of the fresh nuts she used to find in
the wood.

O, how she sighed for her little distant
home. And at last, when she had learned to
think that after all she had been very un-
grateful for the pleasures she had left, and
had made up her mind, bad as her lot was, to
try and be content with it, the little shepherd-
boy's sister begged him so hard to let her set
the little mouse free, that having already
grown tired of it he gave her leave to do as
she liked. And being a very kind little girl,
she thought the pleasant green wood hard by
must be a charming place for a little mouse.
So she asked her mother's leave, and, one
lovely morning, she set out with the dismal
cage in her hand; and away she went far
into the green fields, till she came to one of
the sweetest spots where the blue-bells made
a bright carpet on the ground, and there she

7

opened the cage-door and let loose the **trem-bling** little mouse.

Afraid and bewildered, **it** ran eagerly to the first shelter it could find from the watchful eyes of its kind little friend; but who shall tell its joy when it found itself once more in its own bed of moss. Yes, in **the** very same, under the old oak tree. Its little heart beat with a joy so great that it was almost like pain; and when the little girl was gone, and it peeped out once more and **saw** all the dear well-known scene that had once been so tiresome, it felt that there was no such lovely place in all the world. And, with a grateful heart, it once more took up its abode in the mossy nest, and never again went out of sight of the old oak tree, lest it should lose forever a home the value of which it had *now* fully learned.

CONSCIENCE.

A LITTLE boy called **Jem** Roberts, having been set to weed in a gentleman's garden, observing some very beautiful looking fruit on a tree which grew upon a wall, was strongly tempted to pluck one.

If it tastes but half as nice as it looks, thought he, how delightful it must be! He stood for an instant gazing on the tree, while his mother's words, Touch nothing that does not belong to you, came vividly to mind. He withdrew his eyes from the tempting object, and with great diligence pursued his occupation. The fruit was forgotten, and with pleasure he now perceived he had nearly reached the end of the bed which he had been ordered to clear. Collecting in his hands the heap of weeds he had laid beside him, he returned to deposit them in the wheelbarrow which stood near the peach tree. Again the glowing fruit

met his eye, more beautiful and more tempting than ever, for he was hot and thirsty.
He stood still—his heart beat—his mother's
command was heard no more—his resolution
was gone! He looked around, there was no
one but himself in the garden. They can
never miss one out of so many, said he to
himself. He made a step, only one, he was
now within reach of the prize: he darted forth
his hand to seize it, when at the very moment
a sparrow from a neighbouring tree, calling
to its companion, seemed to his startled ear to
say, Jem, Jem. He sprang back upon the
walk, his hand fell to his side, his whole frame
shook; and no sooner had he recovered himself, than he fled from the spot.

In a short time afterwards he began thus
to reason with himself: "If a sparrow could
frighten me thus, I may be sure that what
I was going to do was very wicked."

And now he worked with greater diligence

than ever, nor once again trusted himself to gaze on the fruit which had so nearly led him to commit so great a fault. The sparrows chirped again as he was leaving the garden, but he no longer fled at the sound.

"You may cry, Jem, Jem," said he, looking steadily at the tree in which several were perched, "as often as you like; I don't care for you now; but this I will say—I will never forget how good a friend one of you has been to me, and I will rob none of your nests again."

THE ORPHAN BOY'S TALE.

STAY, lady, stay, for mercy's sake,
    And hear a helpless orphan's tale,
Ah! sure my looks must pity wake,
    'Tis want that makes my cheek so pale.
Yet I was once a mother's pride,
    And my brave father's hope and joy;

But in the Nile's proud fight he died,
   And **I am** now an orphan boy.

Poor foolish child! how pleased was **I**
   When news of Nelson's victory came,
Along the crowded streets to fly,
   And see the lighted windows flame!
To force me home my mother sought,
   She could not bear to see my joy;
For with my father's life 'twas bought,
   And made **me a** poor orphan boy.

The people's shouts were long **and** loud,
   My mother, shuddering, closed her ears;
"Rejoice! rejoice!" still cried the crowd;
   My mother answered with her tears.
"Why are you crying thus," said I,
   "While others laugh and shout with joy?"
She kissed me—and with such a sigh!
   She called me her poor orphan boy.

"What is an orphan boy?" I cried,
　　As in her face I looked, and smiled;
My mother through her tears replied,
　　"You'll know too soon, ill-fated child!"
And now they've tolled my mother's knell,
　　And I'm no more a parent's joy;
O lady I have learned too well
　　What 'tis to be an orphan boy!

Oh! were I by your bounty fed!
　　Nay, gentle lady, do not chide—
Trust me, I mean to earn my bread;
　　The sailor's orphan boy has pride.
Lady, you weep!—ha?—this to me?
　　You'll give me clothing, food, employ?
Look down, dear parents! look, and see
　　Your happy, happy orphan boy!

AMY'S GARDEN.

Amy lived with her parents in the large house which you see in the picture. There were many pleasant things in and around the house to make the little girl's life happy, but the one which Amy prized most was her garden. Her mamma gave her a round patch in front of the house, and told her she might make a garden there for herself. You can see it in the picture. Her kind brother Rupert dug it all up for her, and showed her how to plant slips and cuttings, and to sow the seeds. And she has now the gayest little patch in the whole large garden before her mamma's house.

There is a border of white pinks and lavender all round. One small bed of white and red roses. Some geraniums and verbena in a little wire basket, round which climbs the bright yellow canariensis. And numbers of annuals and bulbous roots, which bloom in due season and make the place always bright.

And in the centre are some tall hollyhocks and dahlias, under which the sweetest strawberries blossom and ripen. And these Amy gathers, with a glad heart and eager hand, for her papa and mamma, and dear brother who has helped her so kindly. Not one weed is to be seen, the little gardener is so careful.

But, though she loves her garden so much, she does not neglect any other duty to attend to it. But, since she has had it, she gets up

an hour earlier every morning; and that is
the sweetest time of all for working out of
doors. All is so fresh and lovely. All is so
peaceful and still. Except the joyful song
of the little birds that welcome in the new
day.

THE CLEVER BOY.

ONE OF RANDY THE WOODCUTTER'S FABLES,

BY MRS. S. C. HALL.

"WELL, but grandmamma!" expostulated
Edwin, "everybody says I am very clever;—
now do not laugh, everybody says so, and
what everybody says must be true."

"First," replied his grandmother, "I do not
think that what everybody says must of ne-
cessity be true; and, secondly, in what con-
sists your 'everybody?'"

"Why, there is nurse."

"Capital authority! an old woman who

nursed your mother, and, consequently, loves *you* dearly; go on."

"And the doctor;—he said I was so clever, the other morning, when I swallowed the pill without one crooked face."

"Go on."

"All the servants."

"Excellent servants, Edwin, for the situations they are engaged to fill, but bad judges of a young gentleman's cleverness. The Rector——?"

"That is cruel of you, grandmamma," replied our conceited little friend; "you know he would not say it, because I did not get through the Commandment in the class last Wednesday evening."

"Does your papa say you are clever?"

The little fellow made no reply.

"Do your schoolfellows?"

"They are all big boys."

"Then your character for cleverness depends on the old nurse, the still older doctor, and the servants!"

Edwin was again silent.

"This," observed his grandmother, "recalls to my mind one of Randy the Woodcutter's fables."

A very pretty little tree grew near a quick-set hedge that was cut close by the gardener, and the hedge looked up to the tiny little tree with great respect: it was so short itself that it fancied the tree was very tall; there were several brambles and nettles also round about, and they were perpetually praising the little tree, and increasing its vanity by their flattery. One day an old rook, the oldest in the rookery, perched on the little tree.

"What do you mean," said the tiny tree, "by troubling me with your familiarity? the idea of such a bird as you presuming to rest upon my branches!" and the little tree rustled its leaves and looked very angry.

"Caw! Caw!" quoth the rook, which signified, "ah, ah! Why, better trees than you are glad to give me a resting place; I thought you would be gratified by the compliment paid you by alighting on your quivering bough, and by the pleasure of my company; a little thing like you could hardly have possessed much attraction for king rook; but, indeed I only perched upon you because you are a little taller than the brambles."

The dwarf tree considered it as great an insult to be called a "little thing" as some folks do to be considered "not clever;" and he said a number of foolish words; amongst others, that "there were birds that could not fly over him."

"Ay, indeed," answered the rook, "wrens that never mount higher than a hedge!"

The rook soon flew away "caw cawing," at the folly and conceit of the little tree, and meeting the gardener—"Good friend," he said,

"I have just now been much struck by the conceit and absurdity of a little tree beside yonder hedge; it is rather a pretty little thing, and might be brought to something, if it were in the society of trees taller and wiser than itself; but while it has no other companions than brambles and bushes it will never try to grow tall: do, good friend, take pity on this tree, and remove it into better company;" and the gardener had a great respect for the opinion of the old rook, and went the next day with a spade, and removed the turf, and bared the roots of the conceited tree. "It is a stunted little thing," he said, "but I will place it in society that will *draw it up*," and he transplanted it into a plantation where there were straight and noble trees. The little sapling felt bitterly its own insignificance, and its leaves hung helplessly from the boughs; there were neither hedges, nor brambles, nor nettles to flatter its vanity—nothing to pamper its self-love. There was nothing it could look down on; the woodbine turned to the oak for support, and the wild vine clung around the ash. *Thus*, when the little tree derived no pleasure from looking *down*, it began to look *up;* there was a proud fierce sound amid the leaves of the noble trees, and the breezes carried the sound far and wide. The gardener had planted the little tree where it had plenty of headroom, and a very beautiful beech, which grew near it, said, "Dear me, how you are shooting!" and several of the good-natured trees remarked one to the other, that "their little neighbor seemed determined to grow." This was quite true: when removed from the babble of low-bred flattery, and placed with those that were better and higher than itself, the little tree began to understand that false praise, that is, praise for what is not deserved, is the bitterest of all censures; and all his hope was, that he might grow like all other trees to be useful

according to his kind. One stormy night a
sheep and her lamb sheltered beneath his
branches; that made the tree, now no longer
little, very happy. In a few more years the
gardener laid his hand on his stem and said
to a gentleman who was walking with him,
"See what cultivation—which is the education
of trees—does! this was a little stunted thing;
but the good society of tall saplings drew it
up. See what it is now!"

And another day, when there was a very
high wind, the tree saw an old gray-headed
rook drifting about, and he invited him to
rest, and the rook did so, and the tree recognized the voice of his old friend. "I am happy
to see you grandfather rook," he said—"very
happy to see you—you and yours are quite
welcome to rest on or build your nests among
my branches; but for you, I should have remained as I was, to be fooled and flattered by
brambles now—but I have learned to let acts

and not words tell what I am;" and the old rook "caw cawed" again and again, and signified that he knew the time would come when that very tree would be remarked alike for its vigor and its beauty. And the old rook told the history of the tree, as old people sometimes tell histories, over and over again.

"I am sure he would be very proud if it taught you, my dear, the folly of believing that you are clever, because people who do not understand what cleverness is, say you are so."

8

THE CHINAMAN.

THE Chinaman is a native of China. Get your map of the Eastern Hemisphere and see if you can put your finger upon China. It would take many weeks, sailing in swift steamships, to go from America to China; and if we went there, we should find it very different from our own dear home. The men have dark yellowish skins, and wear their hair in a long tail behind, all the hair on the top of their head being shaved off. They wear skirts like a woman, and a sort of loose shirt instead of a coat. The women have such little feet that they can scarcely walk at all. When they are little babies the doctor cuts off all their toes, and they grow up with short clubbed feet. How would you like that? I think you would not like your mother to have your feet cut so that you could neither run, skip, nor jump.

Many useful things are brought to us from China in ships—silk, shawls, fans, spices, and tea.

The Tea-plant is a native of China, where it grows wild, but the Chinese know the value of it too well not to bestow great care on it. They sow the seeds, and when the plants come up, they transplant them in neat rows in large fields; but it is three years before the leaves are fit to use. About March, in the third year, the first half-formed tender leaves are plucked one by one, and are of such great value, that they are kept for the Emperor of China; in April, the second crop is pulled, which is the best tea sent out of China; and in June, the last full-grown thick leaves, which are the coarse rough tea, are gathered. The leaves are first dried in the sun, and then on a heated plate of iron till they shrivel and curl; then the leaves are packed in chests, to be sent off in ships.

The ships carry them across the ocean, and bring them to our country, where you buy them of the grocer.

When you drink your next cup of tea you will think of the work that had to be performed before it reached you, and of the many days the poor Chinaman had to work in the hot sun before the leaves were ready to send across the sea.

THE WILFUL BOY.

"It blew a tremendous gale last night," exclaimed Mr. Thompson to his son William, as he entered the breakfast-room; "I fear we shall hear of great damage done to the shipping."

"Jones has just told me," replied William, "that there are two brigs on the sands near the Goodwin light; and only think, papa, that noble vessel, which sailed with the morning tide yesterday, is totally wrecked! She, too, was driven on the sands in the course of the night; and though it seems she succeeded in getting off, she was so much injured that she almost immediately afterwards went to pieces, and nearly all on board perished with her."

"Put on your hat," said Mr. Thompson, "and we will walk to the pier; we shall get back before your mamma is ready for breakfast."

William instantly did as he was bid—not

that it was his usual custom to do so ; for, like
many other little boys, he **was** very head-
strong, and too often preferred doing what he
liked himself to obeying his parents. Curios-
ity now prompted obedience, and **he was by**
his father's side without the slightest delay.

No sooner had they reached the harbor
than a fearful sight presented itself. The sea
was still violently agitated, and the waves
continued to dash over the end and sides of
the pier, while the wind, still blowing with
strong gusts, rendered standing almost impossible. All was bustle and anxiety; the sailors and fishermen were passing to and fro,
too much occupied by their own thoughts to
heed the questions which the mere spectators
put to them. Several dead bodies lay extend-
ed on the pier head. William shuddered. " O
pray let us go home," exclaimed he ; but before his father could make any reply, the attention of both was attracted by the piercing

lamentations of a poor woman, who was kneeling by the side of a boy, apparently about twelve years old, and who was wringing her hands in an agony of distress.

"O Ned, Ned!" she sobbed, "and is it come to this?" then again and again she repeated, "but he would always have his own way."

Mr. Thompson, turning to one of the bystanders, asked an explanation of the unhappy mother's words.

"I don't like to speak ill of any one," said the fisherman to whom he addressed himself, "and especially of them who can no longer defend themselves: but, if the truth must be spoken, the poor boy that lies there was always a sad, wilful lad, who would have his own way, come what would of it. He was very anxious to go to sea; but neither his father nor mother was willing he should, for he was their only child, and not very strong. All they said, however, was of no use—nay, perhaps, for that is the case with all obstinate, self-willed people, it made him still more determined to have his own way. So yesterday morning, when his father was still away with the mackerel boats, he got on board the 'Resolution' and sailed before any one knew any thing about the matter. His mother was looking for him, half distracted, all the day, and has been on the pier the greater part of the night. His dead body has just been hauled up with several others that you see there."

William again grasped his father's hand, and, hearing another shriek, drew him from the spot. "I cannot, indeed I cannot stay any longer," cried he. Mr. Thompson obeyed his motion; they walked quickly away, nor was a single word spoken by either till they reached the house. Mrs. Thompson was waiting breakfast for them. William sat down in silence, but the expression of his countenance having caught the attention of his mother, she anxiously asked what was the matter. William returned no answer, but, rising from his seat, he threw his arms around her neck, and burst into a violent flood of tears.

"O mamma!" sobbed he, as soon as he could speak, "I have seen such a sight! I have heard such cries! O, I shall never forget them," and he shuddered at the recollection. "Forgive me," he continued passionately, "for being so naughty and obstinate as I know I have often been. Forgive me now; and never, never, will I try to have my own way again, and disobey you."

Mrs. Thompson looked at her husband, who, in a few words, explained what had occurred.

"Thus," said he, as he concluded his distressing story, "thus has God thought fit, in the instance before us, to punish the breach of his holy commandment—'Honour thy father and thy mother, that thy days may be long in the land.' The sea, by his permission, has swallowed up the disobedient child almost in sight of his home; and made his fate **an** awful warning to all who, like him, are tempted to forget the great and sacred duty they owe to their **parents."**

THE GRIZZLY BEAR.

Is he not **a savage** looking beast, as he stands so still, with his big eyes looking so fierce and bright? I wonder what he sees below him, that makes him look so hungry; perhaps, after all, it is only his baby bears at play, and he is growling out to them a caution not to be too rough.

The Grizzly Bear is a native of our own country, and is found in the Rocky Mountains. He is the largest and most savage of the whole bear family, and will attack both men and animals. He is so strong that he can pull down the great buffalo as easily as you lift your kitten from the floor. His large paws have long sharp claws, and when he has once fastened these in man or beast, nothing but death will make him let go his hold.

It is very dangerous to hunt these bears, as the hunter must climb high mountains and risk his life in many ways before he reaches their dens. But their skin and fat are very valuable, so they are often hunted both by white men and Indians. Before the white men came to America, the Indians used the bear skins for blankets and mats, but now they sell them for whiskey, food, beads, nails, and sometimes money, to the whites, who use both the fur and skins.

THE PET FROGS.

ALMOST all children are fond of pets, and I dare say many of my young readers have a pet of some sort, a canary, dog, pony, or rabbit, some pretty animal or bird to feed and caress. I am going to tell you about a boy who had three pet frogs. You may, perhaps, say, What ugly pets! but you are mistaken. The next time you are near a pond, catch a frog and examine it. It will not hurt you; be sure you do not hurt it. When you have looked at it carefully put it down and watch its movements, and I am sure you will find something to ad-

mire both in its looks and actions. But you
will say, perhaps, that frogs are not so inter-
esting as birds, and that they can do nothing
to make you like them: you may say, also,
that they can neither sing nor do any thing
else to please you; but I say, this will depend
upon whether you take an interest in them or
not. You will say, perhaps, that you could
never teach a frog any thing, and that it
would never know you; but I know a youth
who was a little boy nine years ago; and
about that time, while rambling in the pleasant fields, he caught three small frogs and carried them home with him. When he got
home his father and mother thought he had
made a very strange choice in selecting three
such uncommon pets; but they did not for-
bid him to keep them, for he was a very kind
boy, and never hurt any thing.

Well, this little boy kept his three little
frogs in a fishing-can for some time, and put

some grass in with them, and they seemed happy enough; but he could not see them eat any thing, and he thought they would be starved, and this he could not think of without pain, and yet he did not like to take them back again to their native fields, so he thought that he would let them have an opportunity of feeding themselves.

He dug a small pond in his father's garden, not much bigger than a wash-hand basin, which he lined well with clay. At one side of this pond he made a small cave as a sort of apartment, and covered it over with earth. He next got some grass turf and made a grass plot round the pond, and finally, having filled the pond with water, and sprinkled some loose blades of grass on the surface, he put the three young strangers into it, one by one. Before he put them in, however, he gave them names; the largest he called Dick, the next he called Bessy, and the third he called Fanny. Master Dick he put at the edge of the pond, and plump he went to the bottom instantly, and there he lay quiet enough. Next, Miss Bessy was released from the tin can, and plump she went to the bottom also. Next it came to the turn of Miss Fanny, but she was very little and very much wanting in experience, and she knew not what was good for her, so she started off and went hopping about the garden like a grasshopper. Away went the little boy after her, dipping down his hand every second to catch her; but she was too active and quick-sighted for him; away she went and leaped into the middle of a large tulip bed, where she seemed to think herself safe. The little boy respected his father's tulips and did not know how to remove Miss Fanny; but he wished very much to put her with her companions, so he got a long stick and gently touched her. Off she started again, with increased vigor from the

rest she had taken, and the little boy after her.
At length he thought he was sure of having
her, and made a stoop to catch her, but missing his aim, he fell among a number of carnation pots, broke the carnations, and scratched
his face sadly with the carnation sticks.
Well, this little boy was much vexed at the
mischief he had done, and forgot all about
Miss Fanny, and she went he knew not where.
He fixed the carnation sticks in the pots
again, and, having removed the **broken** stems
and put all things in order, he began the
chase afresh; but he looked and looked in
vain—nowhere could he see Miss Fanny. At
last he gave up the pursuit and returned to his
little pond. He was much pleased, however,
when he got there, to see Master Dick and
Miss Bessy peeping their **heads** out at the
edge. When he saw them, **he** thought within himself, how much wiser they were than
silly Fanny; and having left them all safe, he

went to bed, quite pleased with the afternoon's pleasure.

When this little boy awoke in the morning, which was very early, for he was fond of
seeing many things that can be seen only by
early rising, he went to his frog pond to in-
spect his amphibious family, You know, I
hope, my children, that amphibious means
any animal that can live either in the water
or on land. When he came to the pond he
saw no signs of the frogs; he gently moved
the floating grass on one side, but they were
not at the bottom, so he concluded they had
either gone abroad in the garden, or else that
they had concealed themselves in the subter-
ranean cavern. So he waited patiently till
evening came, and then renewed his visit.
He walked gently up to the pond and looked
cautiously into it; and sure enough there
were his three friends, Dick, Bessy, and Fanny,
all sticking their heads out of the water, as if

9

looking for their breakfasts; but, when **they** saw him, plump they went to the bottom.

Many and many were the visits he paid to these queer little things without being able to make acquaintance with them: they seemed too shy for much familiarity.

But one morning, after there **had** been some rain in the night, he went forth as usual, and lo and behold, there he met all three coming home across the garden. He thought he would make free with them, and after one or two trials he caught Master Dick, and taking him into his hand, caressed him, and smoothed him gently with the soft leaf of a rose campion plant, which he happened to have in his hand. Master Dick did not make much effort to get away, but seemed to be pleased. Many and many times, and for several years, did this little boy render himself thus familiar with the frogs; first one and then another, and at length they all became quite tame, and when he came near, they did not jump into the pond as they had done at first, but remained outside, and looked boldly up at him, as much as to say, "Good morning, or good evening, sir," though they would instantly rush into the water if any one else came near them.

The frogs seemed to know his voice, and when he stood still they would sometimes get on to his shoe, as if in full confidence of his kindness.

Nine years have now passed since little Master Dick, little Miss Bessy, and little Miss Fanny first became the property by capture of this little boy. But the little boy has now become a tall youth, and Dick has become a full-grown gentleman frog, and Miss Bessy and the giddy Miss Fanny, two fine handsome full-grown lady frogs. And they are all on the same friendly footing, except that the youth having started in the world to obtain his support has become somewhat a stranger. But there the frogs are still, tenants at will, and there they are likely to remain at present.

Now, my little friends, how do you like frogs by this time? They are not nasty ugly things, are they? I am sure you will say "No." And I wish you to look upon all things with the same interest and good feeling. You will find your walks so pleasant when in the country, if you find an old acquaintance, as it were, in every living thing and plant.

AN INDIAN WIGWAM.

ALL my little readers have heard of
Indians, the red men who lived in this country
before the white men came to drive them

away; but perhaps **there is** some little boy or **girl** who would like to hear more about these **poor** red men of the forest.

At the time when Christopher Columbus discovered America the whole **of** this vast country was inhabited by Indians. **Now**, great cities stand where these savages once hunted the moose and deer, and the poor red man has been driven further and further away from his **old** home, till now there is scarcely one **of** them to be found east of the Mississippi River.

When the Indians were powerful they were very fond of war. Before they went to **war** they would paint their bodies, and string shells and stones round their necks and arms, put gay feathers in their hair, and tattoo their faces. Tattooing is pricking the skin **in** patterns, and then filling the little holes with paint.

While the men dressed so gaily and went to war, the women were not allowed any finery, but were forced to stay at home and cook, draw the water and tend the papooses or babies, which they carried strapped to their backs. If they found any pretty shell or stone they did not dare to wear it, but carried it to the men to make them finer.

As the Indians never lived very long in one place, they never built houses such as we live in, but made themselves wigwams. A wigwam was a number of sticks driven into the ground, and covered with bark leather and branches of trees. In the picture you can see their form. The Indian you see is taking his ease, lying on the ground and smoking his pipe, while his wife cooks the dinner at the fire you see by the tent. The little brown boy has found his father's bow, and struts about in high glee, while the papoose, just taken from his mother's back, is propped up in his queer cradle against the wigwam.

THE WORSTED STOCKING.

A TRUE STORY.

"Father will have done the great chimney to-night, won't he, mother?" said little Tom Howard as he stood waiting for his **father's** breakfast, which he carried to him at his work every morning.

"He said he hoped all the scaffolding would be down to-night," answered the mother, "and this will be a fine sight; for I never like the ending of those great chimneys—it's risky—thy father's to be the **last up.**"

"Eh! then, but I'll go and see him, and help 'em give a shout afore he comes down," said Tom.

"And then," continued his mother, "if all goes right, we are to have a frolic to-morrow, and **go** into the country, and take our dinners, and spend all the day amongst the woods."

"Hurrah!" cried Tom, as he ran off to his

father's place of work, with a can of milk in one hand, and some bread in the other. His mother stood in the door watching him as he went merrily whistling down the street; and then she thought of the dear father he was going to, and then her heart sought its sure refuge, and she prayed to God to protect and bless her treasures.

Tom, with light heart, pursued his way to his father, and leaving him his breakfast went to his own work, which was at some distance. In the evening, on his way home, he went round to see how his father was getting on. James Howard, the father, and a number of other workmen, had been building one of those lofty chimneys which, in our great manufacturing towns, almost supply the place of other architectural beauty. This chimney was one of the highest and most tapering that had ever been erected; and as Tom, shading his eyes from the slanting rays of the setting sun,

looked up to the top in search of his father,
his heart almost sunk within him at the **ap-**
palling height. The scaffold was almost all
down; the men at the bottom were removing
the last beams and poles. Tom's father stood
alone on the top. He looked around to see
that every thing was right; and then waving
his hat in the air, the men below answered
him with a long loud cheer; little Tom shout-
ing as heartily as any of them. As their
voices died away, however, they heard a very
different sound—a cry of alarm and horror
from above! "The rope! the rope!" The
men looked round, and, coiled upon the ground,
lay the rope, which, before the scaffolding was
removed, should have been fastened to the top
of the chimney, for Tom's father to come down
by! The scaffolding had been taken down
without remembering to take the rope up.
There was a dead silence. They all knew it
was impossible to throw the rope up high

enough, or skilfully enough, to reach the top of the chimney; or, if possible, it would hardly have been safe. They stood in silent dismay, unable to give any help, or think of any means of safety.

And Tom's father. He walked round and round the little circle, the dizzy height seeming every moment to grow more fearful, and the solid earth further and further from him. In the sudden panic he lost his presence of mind, and his senses almost failed him. He shut his eyes; he felt as if, the next moment, he must be dashed to pieces on the ground below.

The day had passed as industriously and swiftly as usual with Tom's mother at home. She was always busily employed for her husband and children, in some way or other; and to-day she had been harder at work than usual, getting ready for the holiday to-morrow. She had just finished all her preparations, and her thoughts were silently thanking God for her happy home, and for all the blessings of life, when Tom ran in. His face was as white as ashes; and he could hardly get his words out, "Mother! mother! He cannot get down."

"Who, lad? Thy father?" asked his mother.

"They've forgotten to leave him the rope," answered Tom, still scarcely able to speak. His mother started up, horror-struck, and stood for a moment paralyzed; then pressing her hands over her face, as if to shut out the terrible picture, and breathing a prayer to God for help, she rushed out of the house.

When she reached the place where her husband was at work, a crowd had collected round the foot of the chimney, and stood there quite helpless, gazing up with faces full of sorrow. "He says he'll throw himself down," exclaimed they, as Mrs. Howard came up; "he is going to throw himself down."

"Thee munna do that, lad!" cried the wife, with clear, hopeful voice; "thee munna do that. Wait a bit. Take off thy stocking, lad, and unravel it, and let down the thread with a bit of mortar. Dost hear me, Jem?"

The man made a sign of assent, for it seemed as if he could not speak; and taking off his stocking unravelled the worsted thread row after row. The people stood round in breathless silence and suspense, wondering what Tom's mother could be thinking of, and why she sent him in such haste for the carpenter's ball of twine.

"Let down one end of the thread with a bit of stone, and keep fast hold of the other," cried she to her husband. The little thread came waving down the tall chimney, blown hither and thither by the wind; but at last it reached the outstretched hands that were waiting for it. Tom held the ball of string while his mother tied one end of it to the worsted thread.

"Now pull it up slowly," cried she to her husband; and she gradually unwound the string as the worsted drew it gently up. It stopped,— the string had reached her husband. "Now hold the string fast, and pull it up," cried she; and the string grew heavy, and hard to pull; for Tom and his mother had fastened the thick rope to it. They watched it gradually and slowly uncoiling from the ground as the string was drawn higher. There was but one coil left. It had reached the top. "Thank God! thank God!" exclaimed the wife. She hid her face in her hands in silent prayer, and tremblingly rejoiced. The rope was up. The iron to which it should be fastened was there all right; but would her husband be able to make use of them? would not the terror of the past hour have so unnerved him as to prevent him from taking the necessary measures for his safety? She did not know the strength that the sound of her voice, so calm and steadfast, had filled him with—as if the little thread that carried him the hope of life once more, had carried him some portion of that faith in God which nothing ever destroyed or shook in her true heart. She did not know that, as he waited there, the words came over him, "Why art thou cast down, O my soul? and why art thou disquieted within me? Hope thou in God." She lifted up her heart to God for hope and strength. She could do nothing more for her husband; and her heart turned to God, and rested on him as on a rock.

There was a great shout. "He's safe, mother, he's safe," cried little Tom. "Thou'st saved me, Mary," cried her husband, folding her in his arms. "But what ails thee? Thou seem'st more sorry than glad about it." But Mary could not speak; and, if the strong arm of her husband had not held her up, she would have fallen to the ground: the sudden

joy after such great fear, had overcame her.
"Tom," said his father, "let thy mother lean
on thy shoulder, and we will take her home."
And in their happy home they poured forth
their thanks to God for his great goodness;
and their happy life together felt dearer and
holier for the peril it had been in, and for the
nearness that the danger had brought them
unto God. And the holiday next day—was
it not indeed a thanksgiving day?

ON THE SEA.

DEAR papa is on the sea,
      Willie boy!
Dear papa is on the sea,
Winning gold for you and me,
You'll pray for him at my knee,
      Willie boy, Willie boy!

Your papa is good and true,
      Willie boy!
Your papa is good and true,
To your mamma and to you,
He's beloved by all the crew,
      Willie boy, Willie boy!

10

Then pray as here you kneel,
  Willie boy!
Then pray as here you kneel,
That distress he ne'er may feel,
As he guides the sheet and wheel,
  Willie boy, Willie boy!

Should hurricanes arise,
  Willie boy!
Should hurricanes arise,
Lashing seas up to the skies,
May his guide be the ALL WISE,
  Willie boy, Willie boy!

And the tempest's gloomy path,
  Willie boy!
And the tempest's gloomy path,
May he brave its wildest wrath,
While it strews the deep with death,
  Willie boy, Willie boy!

And on wings of mercy borne,
Willie boy!
And on wings of mercy borne,
May he soon and safe return,
To make glad the hearts that mourn,
Willie boy, Willie boy!

LITTLE THINGS.

"OH! how I wish I was a man," said little Henry, laying down his book with a deep sigh.

"And why, my son, do you so earnestly wish to be a man?" said his mother.

"Because I would like to do some great actions and be useful to my country, like the men mentioned in this book."

"Those great men were all little boys once," said his mother.

"But, mother, do you think they ever **did** any thing *very useful* when they were boys?"

"I should think it very probable," replied his mother, "as all children can be useful if they try."

"But, mother, *what* can such little boys do? **I am** sure I cannot do any good."

"Perhaps you can if you seek for opportunities, and keep always in your mind the wish to do good **to** others. Never let an occasion, however trifling it may appear, pass by unimproved by at least the *effort* to be of use. I cannot talk with you now, as I must go out; but, if you will walk with me, as **I** am going to make some purchases, perhaps we shall find something *to do*, on our way."

"Oh! yes!" said Henry, as he **ran to get his** cap—looking very doubtful, however, as to *his* ability to do any good.

As Henry and his mother pursued their **walk** there were many things to interest them;

but Henry saw no opportunity to do any act of usefulness for some time. At length he noticed an old gentleman before them, and had remarked to his mother that he seemed very feeble, when a rude boy in passing pushed his cane from his hand and ran on, regardless of the inconvenience he was causing.

Henry sprang forward directly, picked up the cane, and with a very modest bow, returned it to the old man.

"Thank you, my son," said the old man, and his face expressed how sincerely he said, "*thank you*." Henry returned to his mother, whose smile of approval expressed her pleasure at his kind act. She said: "You did not have long to wait for an opportunity of being useful."

"Is that *little thing* being useful, mother?"

"Certainly it is. Have you not spared the old man the pain of stooping for his stick, and given him the pleasure of seeing that *all*

little boys are not regardless of age and in-
firmities?"

As they pursued their way, Henry thought
very seriously of his mother's words, and again
resolved to be watchful for an opportunity of
being of service.

They had reached the window of a large,
elegant toy-shop, and Henry left his mother's
side to look at and admire the beautiful things,
thinking, as most children do, that *all* the
toys would make him very happy. A servant
girl, heavily laden with marketing, **let** fall from
her basket a large fine cantelope. It rolled
away very fast, and finally over the curb-stone
into the street. The poor girl looked worried
and perplexed. Both arms had baskets on
them, and the street was much crowded. Hen-
ry, who was looking round at that moment,
saw her distress and hastened to relieve her
trouble. He picked up the cantelope, placed
it securely in her basket, and without waiting

to hear the many thanks which the warm-hearted Irish girl poured upon him, returned to his mother, who again smiled upon him without making any remark. They now turned into another street, and Henry said, " Mother, shall we soon go home, I am so very hungry ? "

" Yes, my dear ; but if you need something to eat, you may step to that cake-baker's on the other side and get yourself a cake, while I make my purchases in this drygoods store ; and then you can return for me. Here are some pennies."

Henry took the pennies and his mother passed into the store, while he skipped away to buy his cake. Henry's mother had finished her business before he returned.

" Well, my son, are you ready to go home ? I have now made all my purchases."

" Yes, mother," replied Henry.

" And how did you like your cake."

"I did not buy one, mother," said Henry.

"Why not?" asked his mother. "I hope you have not **been** buying candy, which you know I do not like you to eat."

"No, mother, I did not buy candy. I saw a little match-girl looking very tired and very hungry, and I gave her my pennies. I knew I should have a nice dinner at home, and I **do not** think she will."

"Another *little good*," said his mother. "Do you not begin to realize that even little boys may be useful when they try."

As they pursued their walk, Henry's mother talked to him about usefulness. "You know, my son, that it is not sufficient that we *wish* to do good; we must be *actively* useful, we must be constantly seeking for opportunities for use. To help our fellow creatures in every way we can is well pleasing to the Lord, who tells us in his Holy Word, to love our neighbors as ourselves. Even high and holy thoughts do not benefit mankind unless there is some channel open for them to flow into *act-ive* use. The hermit in his cell may have pure and holy thoughts, but he does no good to his fellow men by *thinking* good things. They must be brought into *action* to be of *use*. But here we are at home, and now must stop talking."

Henry's mother went directly to the nurs-ery on their return, and he followed her as soon as he had hung up his cap. He found his little darling brother laughing with great glee to see his mother again. Henry had a frolic with him, and then took his book to continue his reading, which his walk had interrupted. His mother was obliged to send the nurse down stairs for a little while, and in a few minutes was herself called down to see the man who had brought home her pur-chases. She placed the baby on the floor and left the room. Henry was much engaged with his book, but when he heard the baby fret at being left, he quietly laid down his book and devoted himself to amusing the little fellow. When his mother returned she kissed him affectionately, and asked him if he still thought it *impossible* for little boys to be useful. "You see, my son, you have had *four* different opportunities of doing acts of kindness, which is but another name for being *useful.* If children desire to be truly good men and women, they must begin, *while children,* to do every good which is in their power, and the "little things" thus done may exercise a power over their whole after lives."

If Henry *could* have known all the good his little actions had done, he would have been convinced that it was in the power of children to be useful. The old man, when he returned home, took his little grandson on his knee, and told him of the good little boy who had picked up his cane, and *he,* too, resolved when he went out to help all the old

people he could see. The small seed was sown
to bring forth, perhaps, much fruit. The
Irish girl, disheartened and fatigued with her
heavy burden, forgot her troubles while telling her fellow servants of the sweet boy with
his sunny face who had run into the street to
pick up her cantelope. The poor little match-
girl made her sick mother's eyes brighten with
pleasure, when she brought to her two beautiful peaches which Henry's gift enabled her
to purchase; and the little baby's look of love
at his brother, who left his book to play with
him, was worth a thousand selfish pleasures.
Henry's mother kept constantly reminding
him that little boys would, in time, become
men, and that for the present he must be con-
tented with "little things," and remember
that the Holy Word says, that "As thy day
is, so shall thy strength be."

THE BALLOON.

BALLOON.

Did you ever see a balloon? It is a large silk bag filled with gas, and covered with strong netting. Suspended from it is a car, in which the people who wish to take a ride in the air can take a seat. When they are seated, the strings which fasten the balloon to the earth are cut, and the gas in the balloon being lighter than the air, it rises up, up far above the ground, floating like a huge bird, till it goes far into the clouds, quite out of sight. In the picture you see a balloon, which is already in the air, and in the car you see the four men who are having a ride.

It is very pleasant to sail through the air in this way, looking down upon trees, fields, cities, mountains, rivers, and plains; but like many other pleasant things, it is sometimes very dangerous. If the bag breaks and lets gas escape, the balloon falls instantly. Some men once started to fly over Lake Erie in a balloon; when they were a short distance from land, the bag burst, the gas rushed out, and the car fell down into the water. There were people on the shore watching, and a man was sent out in a boat, who picked up the half-drowned travellers. Another party, filling the car with provisions, started from Pennsylvania to cross the ocean and fly over to Europe; but when the balloon got as far as New Jersey, the gas began to escape, and the travellers were obliged to come down, very thankful that they were over land instead of being in the middle of the ocean.

———

A STORY OF CHRISTMAS.

"MOTHER! will the Christ-child come to-morrow? Will the Christ-child bring dolls, and horses? and oh, mother, do you think he will bring me a cross-bow, and will Uncle Karl teach me how to shoot it? Mother! why are you so sad? why do your eyes look far away, instead of at Karl? Why do you not answer me, mother?"

"Karl!" said the mother, drawing him closely to her breast, "do you love me?"

"Love you? Why, mother, what a question! I love you most dearly, dear mother."

"You will never leave me, my boy?"

"Never, dear mother! Why should I leave you?"

"Never, never leave me."

"Gertrude," said a low voice behind her chair.

The boy slid down from his mother's lap, and left her alone with his father.

"Oh, my husband," cried the wife, laying her head on his breast, "my heart is sad to-night, and over-weary. Where is our boy, our first-born?"

"Gertrude, he left us freely; he was head-strong, and unwilling to submit to his father's better judgment. God protect him, for he was young and wayward. I know not where he is, though half my fortune has been spent in vain endeavors to find him. Our poor boy! he may be dead, Gertrude."

The mother shuddered. **Then** rising, she went to a drawer and took out a cross-bow, and some other boyish toys, and laid them apart. Her hand lingered lovingly over them, and the tears welled up into her eyes.

"They are for Karl," she said in answer to her husband's look of inquiry. "It is five years to-morrow since I placed them on the tree for Emanuel, and in two little weeks I saw my boy for the last time. I have tried always to banish sad thoughts at Christmas, for the children's sake, but to-night my heart seems full enough to burst. God grant we hear of no misfortune happening to our boy, for **my** heart has heavy forebodings."

Long did the parents sit and talk of the prodigal son.

Emanuel was their first, and for five years after their marriage, their only child. He was a high-tempered boy, but until his thirteenth year had submitted to his parents' will. One night, in a sudden fit of rage at the crossing of some unreasonable whim, he had left the house, walked to a neighboring seaport town, and there taken passage on a vessel bound for China. As this vessel sailed the next morning, with its new cabin-boy on board, every effort made by his father to bring him back had been fruitless. For some time the mother was prostrated by grief, but other children claimed her attention, and as their childish wonder abated, and they ceased to mention their brother's name, it was not spoken in the family circle, and the parents slowly learned to shut up this great sorrow in their own hearts.

The morrow came, and with a sad face and many a falling tear, Gertrude placed Emanuel's toys on the tree for Karl. If he ever returned, the mother lovingly argued, he would be too old for these trifling gifts, and they would

11

make her Karl happy. Dancing feet and merry voices greeting her, as she left the mysterious room she had prepared for the Christ-child, soothed the open wound in her heart, and she thanked God for the treasures left to her.

Evening came; the children, **Karl,** Fritz, Gertie, Franz, and little Dorothea were all ushered into a dark entry, and there joined their sweet childish voices in **the** Christmas-hymn. Then the door opened, and in a **won-**drous blaze of light stood the Christmas tree. Awe-stricken by its glorious light, **and** dazzled by its suddenness, the children stood still, until seeing grandmother, whose chair had been wheeled in, sitting by a table near this burst of splendor, they came slowly in. Karl's quick eye soon espied his treasure, **the cross-**bow, and Uncle Karl was called upon to **ex-**plain all its mysteries. Fritz took his new book to have the pictures explained by grand-mother. **Gertie** sat beside the table with a new doll, while little Franz and the two year old baby, soon tired with intense pleasure, came to papa's loving arms for rest. The mother wandered round the room. Karl's eagerness reminded her of the pleasure the same toy had given five long years before. The book Fritz enjoyed so much was also one of Emanuel's, and as Gertrude's eye turned from one boy to the other, her heart whispered the oft-repeated question, "Will he never return!" There was a shadow on the father's brow too, and as Gertrude passed him, he grasped her hand, and drew her closely to him. All the children were too happy to notice their parents' abstraction, and their low voices were drowned in gleeful shouts and animated conversation.

Suddenly there came a loud rap on the door. Gertie, much wondering whom it could be on Christmas eve, sprang to open it. The mother stood erect, and the father, his heart stirred by the same hope, looked eagerly toward the door. It was a stranger, a lad of eighteen or nineteen years; they looked for a boy of Karl's age, forgetting for a moment the lapse of time. He stood in the doorway, then with a slow, timid step, advanced toward the mother and father. Gertrude's, the mother's instinct, spoke first, and with a loud cry she fell upon his neck.

"Mother! mother!" he said, in a hoarse, choked voice, "can you forgive me?"

"Forgive? Oh, my boy! Heaven is very good to me. Five years I have thirsted for the sound of your voice, and the sight of your face, and God has sent you home."

"Father!"

The father spoke not, but as his son fell at his feet, he bent forward and pressed the seal of forgiveness upon his brow. And the Christmas day rose upon such happiness in that house as it had never known before.

WISHING.

A NURSERY SONG.

Ring-ling! I wish I were a Primrose,
A bright yellow primrose blooming in the
     Spring!
  The stooping boughs above me,
  The wandering bee to love me,
The fern and moss to creep across,
And the Elm-tree for our king!

Nay, stay! I wish I were an Elm-tree,
A great lofty-Elm-tree, with green leaves gay!
  The winds would set them dancing,
  The sun and moonshine glance in,
And birds would house among the boughs,
And sweetly sing!

O no! I wish I were a Robin;
A Robin or a little Wren, everywhere to go!
  Through forest, field, or garden,
  And ask no leave or pardon,

Till winter come with icy thumb,
To ruffle up our wing!

Well, tell! where should I fly to,
Where go to sleep in the dark wood or dell!
  Before a day was over,
  Home must come the rover,
For mother's kiss—sweeter this
Than any other thing.

THE APTERYX.

APTERYX.

TRAVELLERS who have ventured into the wild, unknown parts of Australia, have seen many new animals, all of which have been quite unlike those of other countries. Amongst those which have really been brought to this country, the most curious is the Apteryx, called by the natives *Kiwi-Kiwi*. It is quite without wings, and the nostrils are placed nearly at the end of the very long bill, the tip of which it has a habit of placing on the

ground when it rests. The bird is covered
with soft, hair-like feathers, which are never
plucked out, but the whole skin is used for
the dresses of the chiefs. The legs are very
strong and powerful, and are used to defend
it from the dogs that hunt it; and also to
strike the ground, to force up the worms on
which it feeds. It makes its nest in caves in
the rock, or it digs holes in the earth, in which
it hides when pursued.

MARY THOMPSON.

"PRAY let that tree alone," said a lady,
addressing a little girl about eleven years old,
who was picking off the bark of a fine elm,
that grew near the entrance of a gentleman's
grounds. "Do you not know that what
you are doing is very injurious to the tree?
See," added she, turning to the lady who was

with her, "what a large space has been entirely laid bare."

"I didn't do it," said the girl pertly; "it was there long before I ever touched the tree."

"Probably," replied Miss Sinclair; "but that is no reason why you should make it worse. Leave the tree," said she authoritatively, for the girl still held her hand upon it, nor had moved a single step.

"It's none of yours," exclaimed she, in a tone sufficiently loud for Miss Sinclair to hear, though apparently pronounced for the entertainment of her companions, who began to titter.

"What is that you say?" demanded Miss Sinclair, turning back a few paces.

"I didn't say any thing," replied she.

"What is your name?" demanded Miss Sinclair: but no answer was returned. She then made the same inquiry of the other girls who were with her, one alone of whom made any reply, and that was no further satisfactory than that she gained from it that her name was Mary; whether she went to the school, where she lived, or what was **her** surname, were points her informant professed to know nothing about.

"It is as well for your friends," said Miss Sinclair, "that your name is **not** known; for impertinent children are not less a disgrace to their parents than objects of dislike to others. We may meet again, perhaps, when I shall not forget either your countenance or your words; for an insolent tongue, and a disrespectful manner, seldom fail either to make an impression not easily to be effaced, or to receive some degree of punishment."

The girl spoke not, but her looks sufficiently expressed her inclination again to answer. Miss Sinclair, however, walked on, and soon each was out of sight of the other.

Mary—for as such alone we will for the present know her—was, without any exception, the pertest girl in the village. Let who would speak, she had always an answer to make, and would have the last word, though numbers were present. Her manner, her appearance, the cast of her countenance, every feature, the movement of her shoulders, and the twist of her neck, and—if the expression may be allowed—the very sit of her clothes, and her way of putting on her bonnet, was pert. If her mother happened to say, "I like such and such a thing to be done thus; I think it the better plan;" Mary's head was at once in motion, her lip was raised, and "Do you?" was the reply; and sometimes even she would add, "but I don't." There was no mistaking the meaning of the action at any time; and so her father proved to her one evening, when hearing the words, and catching the expression that accompanied them, he raised the glove he had in his hand, and smartly struck her on **the** shoulder with it.

"Is that the way," said he, angrily, "that you answer your mother? If ever I hear you speak in that manner again you shall have something still more to cry for than you have now." The blow had been sharp, and the pain caused by it severe, and Mary's tears flowed plentifully; yet even in that moment, **so** powerful was the force of habit, that she was on the point of uttering some reply—the determined look of her father, and the glance she caught of his uplifted glove, checked her, and made her thankful to escape.

She was the same at school. Mrs. Davis, the mistress, had more trouble with her on this account, than she had ever experienced from any girl before, and as yet she had found no means of effectually correcting her. This was the more to be regretted, as she was really **a** very "handy" **little** girl, by no means inclined to be idle, and possessed, besides, very good sense.

With her brothers she was no favorite. "Miss Pert" was the name by which they generally distinguished her; and, while quarrels were frequent between them and herself, they rarely invited her to share in any pleasure that they proposed among themselves.

"Mother," said Frank, the eldest boy, "I will take my angle, and see if I can't catch a dish of fish for supper; it is just such an evening when the fish will bite, as fast as I can throw the bait."

"Will they?" said Mary; "I'm glad you think so."

"No one spoke to you, Miss Pert," returned Frank, coloring with passion; "when I want a girl's opinion, I'll ask you for it."

One word of course led to another, and angry words and burning hearts were the consequence.

"O mother!" cried Mary one day when she returned from school, "what do you think Mrs. Davis has been telling us? The lady who has come to live at the Grove keeps a great many pretty birds, birds of *all* sorts, and she wants a little girl to help her to feed them, and attend to them. She is not to live there entirely, but to go at certain times of the day, so that it may not interfere with school-hours: they say she is such a nice lady; and every thing about her is quite beautiful. O mother, I should so like to go to her! Don't you think Mrs. Davis might have spoken a good word for me?"

"*Could* she have spoken a *good* word for you, Mary?" said her mother, looking steadily at her.

"Could she!" repeated Mary, and the tell-tale toss of her head, and jerk of the neck, betrayed that Mrs. Davis's last exhortations and her own promises of amendment were forgotten.

"Mary!" said her mother, in a tone which recalled her to recollection.

She blushed, and in a more becoming manner said, "Will you go with me, mother, and ask the lady to take me?"

Her mother consented; and it was agreed that they should go together in the evening. Seeing both dressed in their Sunday attire, the brothers inquired where they were going. Mary, with some importance, informed them.

"Well, take care," said one of them, "only mind that you leave 'Miss Pert' behind you, and then perhaps you may stand a chance to be nursery-maid to the birds."

"Nursery-maid indeed!" returned Mary; "who cares for such boys as you?" and her little slight figure became in an instant perfectly erect and statue-like, with the exception of the head and neck, which assumed its accustomed movement on such occasions.

"If there is another word spoken," said her mother, "you may go by yourself, for I will not go with you."

"As you please," were the words that hung on Mary's tongue, but she checked the utterance, and in silence they left the house together.

When they reached the Grove they were shown into an apartment and desired to wait; the door which led into an adjoining room was open, so that the voices within were distinctly heard. Mary immediately recognized Mrs. Davis to be the speaker. "There is no one, ma'am," said she, "whom I could so confidently recommend as Mary Thompson, if it were not for the fault that I have mentioned. I am sure she would suit you in every respect; whatever she does she does well, and quickly too; but she has such a tongue! I cannot advise you to take her."

At that instant the lady to whom she was speaking, perceiving the figures of persons in the antechamber, arose and advanced towards it. Addressing Mary's mother as she entered, she inquired her business. Mary stole a look at her, but meeting her eyes, she hastily turned her head away. Had she seen her before? She could hardly tell: her voice certainly did not seem strange to her, yet she could not think when or where she had heard it. Whilst her mother was enumerating her daughter's qualifications, and in natural terms commending her, Mary was amusing herself with looking at some beautiful flowers, which were tastefully arranged in a vase on a small table, near which she was standing. Fearful that she might be taking a liberty, her mother, availing herself of an opportunity, as she thought, of not being observed, shook her

12

head, and by the motion of her lips, rather than by direct utterance, said "Don't do so." But this was enough for Mary. "Not to do so!" she repeated, accompanying the words with the movement of her head so peculiarly her own.

"Mary Thompson!" said the lady, in a voice which made her start, "I require no one to tell me that you are she. Those flowers **are** none of yours—do you now recollect me?"

Mary **was** almost ready to sink on the carpet; she had never before been so completely subdued.

"Miss Pert" was, indeed, left behind. She colored, trembled, and at last burst into tears. Her mother looked at her with astonishment. Miss Sinclair then related what had occurred at their first meeting, to the great distress of the poor woman.

"Mary," said Miss Sinclair, as she concluded her narration, " you may now see both the folly and the danger of impertinence. The conduct shown to a stranger might, without any other knowledge, now deprive you of a very great advantage. Our second meeting, like our first, is by no means calculated to give me a favorable impression of you; but there is no habit altogether so inveterate as not to be conquered by perseverance and determination, and I would much rather be the means of your improvement than of your punishment. You shall come to me, but on this clear understanding—that if you repeat the fault I have thus twice witnessed, you leave me in disgrace, and without any prospect of returning to me."

Mary went home humbled and mortified; but if her brothers are to be believed, "Miss Pert" expired that evening, and though for some time after they had fears of her coming to life again, she has certainly up to this hour been to all intents and purposes dead and buried.

———

HOW BOOKS ARE MADE.

A PRINTING PRESS.

WHEN your dear papa, little reader, brings you home the pretty book that is to give you many pleasant hours, do you ever think of the number of people who have been employed to give you this pleasure. I don't

think you ever stopped a moment to thank
them; so I am going to tell you something
about the manufacture of books, that you
may understand what a large amount of work
it requires to make even the smallest book.

First, then, there is the author, or person
who writes the words for you to read. He
must sit many hours and days, busy with his
pen, to tell you of other countries, or of birds
and beasts, or to write out the pretty stories.
The designer, too, or man who draws the pictures which you like so well, must ply his
pencil, and use his eyes and fingers busily,
before the pretty scenes are ready for you.

The engraver must then take his sharp
little tools, and dig into the hard wood or
steel on which the picture is drawn, until he
has it ready for the paper upon which you see
its impression.

Then comes the printer, to set the type,
and stamp upon the page the words you read.

In the picture you see the press which he uses for this purpose. All the letters are cut in little steel type, then put together to form the words and sentences, and fastened very securely in frames made for that purpose. These frames are then put in the printing press, where the letters are carefully inked. The paper is then laid over them, and pressed down with great force, so that the ink **will** come off upon it, and leave the little black letters.

Then the leaves must be taken by the stitcher and sewed together **to** form the book; the binder takes them next, and puts on the pretty stiff covers which keep the pages neat and clean, and finally the packer sends them to the bookstore where papa finds them out for you.

But even before the book is printed, there are many hours of labor spent upon the materials. The paper employs the ragpicker and manufacturer; the covers require the aid of the leather **or cloth** maker, and gilder; **and the** ink must be made, the press itself manufactured, and many hands employed before one book is ready for you to read. So when you look at a book, you should bear in mind the number **of** persons that have been employed in producing it; and then, perhaps, it will rise in your estimation. There are the author, the designer, the publisher, the rag merchant, the paper maker, the stationer, the type founder, the press maker, the ink maker, the chase maker, the compositor, the pressman, the gatherer, the folder, the stitcher, the the leather seller, the binder, the copper smith, the engraver, the copper plate printer, the bookseller, and many other trades besides. **All** of these require, also, the assistance of persons of other employment, so that no fewer than a hundred people, directly or indirectly, have been occupied in the production of every bound book which is decorated with copper plates or wood cuts.

HOW HARRY DIXON BEGAN TO THINK.

THE family dinner was just over—Mr. Dixon had gone to his workshop—some of the children had run out to play before going to school; but Harry had taken his chair near to the fire, where he sat watching his mother as she cleared the table.

Harry was about ten years old; a good-tempered boy, and a handy little fellow in his way; but like many other boys, he did things without thinking, and so brought himself into trouble. His father often **said that** the young chap had no head, and was of no use to anybody.

When Harry heard his father say this he

always felt unhappy, and wished he could become a useful boy all at once, and so make up for past troubles. His good disposition made him willing to render such services as were in his power; but he did not know how much power of this sort he had, as he ran about playing with his brothers and sisters; and in the fun and frolic a mishap of some kind was pretty sure to happen.

Harry, as we have said, was sitting by the fire; he had done no mischief that day, and felt pretty comfortable as he watched his mother's proceedings. She had nearly done clearing away, when he saw her take up the bread-basket and water-jug with one hand, and with the other a saucepan from the hob, and carry all three at once away to the pantry.

"How clever my mother is," said Harry to himself, "I should never have thought of making one journey do for three things."

Then he sat silent for a time, wondering whether he would one day be able to do the same. He had often heard his mother say, "make your head work for your hands," and now he understood what she meant.

Those few minutes of reflection formed one of the turning points in Harry's history, and for the first time in his life he began to think.

After this, it seemed to Harry that difficulties were not so formidable as heretofore; and he scarcely ever woke in the morning without thinking about what he should do through the day. In this way he found out that it was possible for even a young boy to be very useful at home. One of the first things that he did was to collect all the large stones he could find, and with these he made a pathway across the yard to the ash-pen and water-butt; and this saved the kitchen from a good deal of dirt, especially in wet weather.

He pulled up all the weeds and grass from the garden paths, and made a rule of sweeping them every other day; besides which he mended the fence, and put a new hasp to the gate. He found time, too, to keep the books in tidy order on the shelves; and, setting his wits to work, he contrived to put a new leg to the washing-stool, and to mend the broken rails of the kitchen chairs. In short, Harry found that when people are willing to be useful they can do almost any thing, and he would never have believed, had he not proved it, that so much could be done in a day. He did not give up play, but by making his head work, he gained time for work as well as play. He had not only the satisfaction arising from a true desire to do his duty, but he gained the approbation of his parents: his mother often looked after him as he ran off to school, with a glad eye and thankful heart, that her young son was such a comfort to her.

[Our youthful readers must not suppose that this is a tale merely made up for the occasion; it is a true history. Harry is now an old man, yet he can still look back with satisfaction to the time when he began to think.]

AN AQUARIUM.

AQUARIUM.

Is not this a pretty aquarium? An aquarium is a glass vessel, or tank filled with water, sea weed, pebbles, shells, and fishes. They are sometimes very large, sometimes small enough to stand on a little table. When well filled and the water kept clear, they are very beautiful; and it is a very pleasant way of passing an hour or two, to watch the little fish as they dart in an out among the weeds.

My brother once had an aquarium of which he was very proud; **he** had carefully washed the pretty white san**d**, and spread it over the bottom of his tank; had spent many days **in** hunting for the weeds and pebbles, and begged from his mother some beautiful shells. All the fish were caught by his own net, on holidays, and his pretty treasure was his favorite amusement. **One** day while he **was** at school, his little sister, who was just learn**ing to count,** thought **she** would like to know how many fish there **were** in Charley's aquarium. So she took the little net with which Charley removed the fish to a bucket of water when he cleaned the tank, and carefully lifted out all the fish. But Lizzie did not know that fish will not live out of water, and she spread them all out on the carpet. At first they struggled and gasped, then lay quite still. As Lizzie could not count as far as five, she divided the fish into little heaps, five in each heap, and then went to Charley to know how many five heaps of five fishes each, made. Can you tell?

Poor Charley! As soon as Lizzie told him what she had done, he ran hastily into the room, to see all his little pets lying dead on the carpet.

"Oh, Lizzie! You've killed all my fish!"

Lizzie stood a moment very still, looking at the mischief she had done, and then began to cry bitterly.

"Oh, Charley! Are they dead? The poor little fish! Oh, I did not mean to kill them. I lifted them out very carefully."

"But they will not live out of the water."

"But, Charley, they would not keep still while I counted them! Oh, I am so sorry!"

Now Charley was a kind-hearted little

boy, and when he saw how grieved and sorry his little sister was, he began to comfort her.

"Never mind, Lizzie, there are plenty more fish in the river. I will catch some more on Saturday, and I am sure you will not touch them."

Lizzie promised never to touch the tank again, and kept her promise.

Now was not this much better than if Charley had been passionate, and scolded his little sister? Lizzie learned to be more careful about touching what did not belong to her, and loved her gentle brother more dearly than ever.

THAT IS A BOY I CAN TRUST.

"I once visited," says a gentleman, "a large public school. At recess a little fellow came up and spoke to the master; and as he turned to go down the platform, the master said, ' *That is a boy I can trust.* **He** *never* **failed me.'** I followed him with my eye, and looked at him when he took his seat after recess. He had a fine, open, manly face. **I** thought **a good** deal about **the** master's remark. What a character had that little boy earned! **He** had already got what would be worth to him more than a fortune. It would be a passport to the best office in the city, and what is better, to the confidence **of all. I** wonder if the boys know how soon they are *rated* by older people. Every boy in the neighborhood is known, and opinions formed of him; **he has a** character, either favorable **or** unfavorable. **A boy of** whom **the** master **can** say, 'I can trust **him**; he *never* failed me,' will never want employment. The fidelity, promptness, and industry which he has shown at school are prized everywhere. He who is **faithless in** little shall be faithless in much.''

13

THE BAD CLOCK.

I HAVE a clock on my parlor mantelpiece. A very pretty little clock it is, with a gilt frame, and a glass case to cover it. Almost every one who sees it, says, "What a pretty clock!" But it has one great defect—it will not run; and therefore, as a *clock*, it is perfectly useless. Though it is very pretty, it is a bad clock, because it never tells what time it is.

Now, my bad clock is like a great many persons in the world. Just as my clock does not answer the purpose for which it was made —that is, to keep time—so, many *persons* do not answer the purpose for which they were made. What did God make us for? "Why," you will say, "He made us that we might love Him and serve Him." Well, then, if we do *not* love God and serve Him, we do not answer the purpose for which He made us:

we may be, like the clock, very pretty, and be very kind, and very obliging; but if we do not answer the purpose for which God made us, we are just like the clock—bad. Those of my readers who live in the country, and have seen an apple-tree in full blossom, know what a beautiful sight it is. But suppose it only bore blossoms, and did not produce fruit, you would say it is a bad apple-tree. And so it is. Every thing is bad, and every person is bad, and every boy and girl is bad, *if they do not answer the purpose for which God made them.* God did not make us only to play and amuse ourselves, but also that we might do His will.

Maybe some of our readers will say, How can I do God's will? I will tell you. It is God's will that you obey your parents. It is His will that you keep out of bad company. It is His will that you always try to do what is right. It is His will that you pray and read your bible. And it is God's will, my dear young friends, that you believe in Jesus Christ, trust in Him for the pardon of your sins, and pray for His Holy Spirit. Now be sure that you try to be *not* like the clock, which, though it is very pretty, is a *bad* one, because it does not answer the purpose for which it was made. Let every one, therefore, ask himself the question, "Do I answer the purpose for which God made me?"

THE GREAT AUK.

THE Great Auk feeds on fish; it is found on all the shores of the Northern Ocean, and is sometimes seen in the Northern Islands of Scotland. Its short wings are of no use in flying, and its legs are so far back that it walks very slowly; but it dives well, and swims under the water, rising at a great dis-

tance from the place where it went down.
The sailors know they are near land when
they see the Great Auk, which never ventures
far from the shore. The plumage of the head,
neck, **and** back **is** black, and the under parts
are white, with a white patch before the eyes.
On the cleft of a high rock this bird lays one
large white egg streaked with purple; and
these eggs are so rare that they are **much**
valued by collectors.

ANDROCLES AND THE LION.

I READ once a story that I think will
please you. It was called Androcles and
the Lion. In those days, when rich people
were served by slaves, whom they could sell
or torture as they pleased, there was a man
named Androcles, who had the misfortune to
be in the service of a hard and cruel master.

And his slavery was at last so bitter to him, that he resolved to run away. But he had no friends, and no other home than that where he lived in bondage. So he could flee nowhere for escape but to the lonely woods. There, hidden amongst pathless wilds, he thought he should be safe from pursuit; and as to the dangers from hunger, or savage beasts that were likely to attack him there, he dreaded them less than the iron rod under which he had been so long groaning. Or perhaps even he did not think of them at all, but only of the liberty after which his heart panted. So, one dark night, he stole away when all the household was asleep, and before the dawn of day was already far off amongst the wilds of a thick forest, which no human foot had ever trod before.

He was well used to hard fare, so the nuts and berries he could find were all-sufficient for his hunger. But after walking deeper and deeper into the forest he began to feel tired, and looking round for some place where he might sleep with safety, he saw very near him a large and rocky cave. This was just the very thing for **poor** Androcles, and going a little way into it, he lay down upon a heap of dry leaves some idle wind had blown there, and was soon fast asleep.

How long he slept he could not tell, but he was at last awakened by a loud moaning, and starting up, what was his horror to see at the entrance of the cave a monstrous lion. This cave was his den, as poor Androcles little thought when **he** took possession of it. Fear almost stopped his breath at first, and he stood trembling, expecting every moment that the **lion** would spring upon him. But strange to say, the great creature showed **no desire** to do so, but only moaned and held up one of its forepaws, which it did not seem able to put to the ground.

Androcles by degrees took heart, and observed that this paw was very much swelled, and certainly in great pain. Whether he found courage to walk to the lion, or whether the lion limped towards him, I do not remember; but I know that at last he thought he would try to help the poor suffering beast, and taking hold of the enormous paw, he saw that a very large thorn was sticking in the ball of the foot. This it was which made the lion in such pain; and some instinct seemed to assure him that Androcles would help him in his trouble, and he sat patiently waiting to see what he would do.

Now Androles was very kind-hearted, and had not been made hard or unfeeling by his own sorrows. So he forgot all his fears in trying to comfort the poor wounded lion, and taking hold of the thorn he very carefully drew it from his foot. No sooner did the lion feel the cause of his suffering taken away than he was filled with joy, and began to jump about, as you may have seen a dog do when it is pleased. Poor Androcles thought that now he should certainly be eaten up; but, to his great surprise, the lion came and fawned upon him, and tried in every way to show his gratitude for the favor he had received.

However, Androcles felt so little at ease, **that** he took the first opportunity of escaping from the den, and going further to find another shelter. But the lion was soon at his side again, and was so gentle and playful and loving, that at last Androcles made up his mind to trust his grateful companion, and they went back together to the den. There for many weeks they lived in the greatest harmony and happiness, and poor Androcles found in the society of the wild beast **a** pleasure he had never tasted in the presence of his fellow men. Every day the lion went out to forage for food, and Androcles always shared his prey which he cooked by means of a fire kindled with flints and dry wood.

But at last the lion was wounded by the hunters while out in search of food, and returning to his den was tracked thither by the blood he shed. There one of the hunters seeing Androcles knew him at once as the slave that had been missed. For he was a valuable slave, and had been sorely wanted by his master ever since his flight, and every thing had been done to find out where he was hidden, but in vain till now. So poor Androcles was carried back to the city he had left, and there being tried before a judge, he was found guilty, and condemned to be thrown to a wild beast ; **for** to run away was the greatest crime a slave could commit, and no punishment was thought too bad for it.

Well, he was put in prison until the day fixed for his death, and then brought into the place where such cruel scenes used to be acted.

And a lion, that had been kept without food for many days on purpose that he might be savagely hungry, was let loose upon him.

Hundreds and hundreds of people were gathered round the **spot** in order to see the dreadful sight ; but what was their wonder when the furious lion, who had sprung eagerly forth on seeing a man ready for him to devour, fell tamely down before Androcles and licked his feet with every sign of gentleness and love. For it was indeed his own forest friend who had been brought to eat **him up** ; but who, hungry though he was, would **not** harm the man who had been so **kind** to him.

The strange story spread far and wide, and soon reached the ears of the governor, who ordered the man and the lion (**who** follow-ed him like **a** dog) to be brought before him. And when **he** had heard Androcles's tale, and seen the wonderful gratitude of the lion, he gave command **that** Androcles should be set at liberty, since the sentence passed upon him, of being exposed to a wild beast, had been complied with, and that the lion should be presented to him for his own.

THE TWO ARTISTS.

Two little boys were once amusing themselves by drawing on their slates, after morning school was over .They were both very fond of drawing, and had lessons from a drawing master twice a week.

"Robert," said Charley, "when I am a man I mean to go to Italy ; there I shall find such models amongst the works of old masters, and the churches, and temples, and other buildings. And papa says the sky is so blue and bright there, that every thing looks as well again as it does in this smoky London ; and I mean to go to Greece too. O, how I shall enjoy myself when I am a man, and can go about and draw all day long. Won't you?"

"I hope I shall enjoy myself," said Robert; "but I do not think I shall go abroad. For, since papa's death, mamma has never liked to let me stay long out of her sight. And, if I went abroad, I should be away from her for a long while."

"No; but think of all you would have to show her when you came home. How happy that would make her!"

"I think," said Robert, "I shall find plenty of beautiful things to draw here. Mamma says there are scenes as lovely here as heart can desire, and she has promised to take me about with her to see my native country when I have left school."

These little boys grew **up**. Charley went abroad, **as** he said he would. And before he went he very earnestly begged Robert to go with him. But Robert said, "I cannot leave

my mother. She is not strong. I should like
to go abroad very much, and above all with you,
dear Charley. But I must not and cannot leave
her." So Charley went, and Robert stayed
with his dear mamma. She grew weaker and
weaker, and they journeyed about from one
lovely English scene to another, and in each
spot Robert made his portfolio rich with
sketches. And Charley profited well by the
advantages he enjoyed. He studied hard at
Rome, and made himself a first-rate artist. One
day, when he had visited Greece and returned
to Rome, he was busy over the details of some
splendid ruins he had been copying, when he
heard a well-known voice behind him, and
turning round he was in the arms of his dear
friend Robert. When the first moment of
delight was over, Charley saw that his friend
was in deep black. He did not like to ask him
the reason in their first joyous meeting; but
when, late in the day, they were sitting looking

over each other's drawings and enjoying the progress each had made, Charley said, "Let me see your last; you have seen mine." Robert put it silently into his friend's hand. It was his mother's grave. "O, Charley," said he at last, bursting into tears, "how thankful I feel now that I never left her."

THE END.

www.ingramcontent.com/pod-product-compliance
Lightning Source LLC
Chambersburg PA
CBHW020620030726
47497CB00007B/2328